shooting the moon

frances o'roark dowell

atheneum books for young readers
new york • london • toronto • sydney

Atheneum Books for Young Readers
An imprint of Simon & Schuster Children's Publishing Division
1230 Avenue of the Americas, New York, New York 10020

Book design by Michael McCartney
The text for this book is set in Impressum.

Manufactured in the United States of America

First Edition
10 9 8 7 6 5 4 3 2 1

Library of Congress Cataloging-in-Publication Data
Dowell, Frances O'Roark.
Shooting the moon / Frances O'Roark Dowell. — 1st ed.
p.   cm.
Summary: When her brother is sent to fight in Vietnam, twelve-year-old
Jamie begins to reconsider the army world that she has grown up in.
ISBN-13: 978-1-4169-2690-0
ISBN-10: 1-4169-2690-9
1. Vietnam War, 1961–1975—United States—Juvenile fiction.
[1. Vietnam War, 1961–1975—United States—Fiction. 2. Military bases—Fiction.
3. Children of military personnel—Fiction. 4. Separation (Psychology)—Fiction.
5. Soldiers—Fiction. 6. United States Army—Fiction.] I. Title.
PZ7.D75455Sh 2008
[Fic]—dc22
2006100347

● shooting the moon ●

For my father,
Brigadier General Dulaney L. O'Roark Jr.,
United States Army, Retired.

And for my mother,
Jane Fowley O'Roark,
who also deserves a star.

ACKNOWLEDGMENTS

The author would like to thank the following
people for their support and encouragement:
Caitlyn M. Dlouhy; Susan Burke;
Clifton, Jack, and Will Dowell;
Amy Graham; Kathryn and Tom Harris;
Virginia Holman; Carie McElveen;
and Danielle Paul.

one

The day after my brother left for Vietnam, me and Private Hollister played thirty-seven hands of gin rummy, and I won twenty-one. They were speedball games, the cards slapped down on the table fast and furious. My brother, TJ, was going to war, and I was fired up hotter than a volcano. TJ and I had grown up in the Army, we were the Colonel's children, but that was not the same as being a soldier in the very heart of combat.

"Whoa, hoss, slow down," was the first thing Private Hollister said when I'd charged into the rec center that morning, ready for action, but not exactly knowing what to do with myself. I'd been a rec center volunteer for three whole days, which had mostly involved picking up crumpled Coke cans from under the pool tables and handing out Ping-Pong paddles to soldiers. But now I couldn't settle myself down enough to go check the chore list on the clipboard Private Hollister kept on his desk. I wanted to spin around in circles, do jumping jacks, drop to the floor for a hundred push-ups. Big things were happening, and the excitement of it all was running through my veins and winding me up tight.

"Here. Sit." Private Hollister pulled out his desk chair and motioned for me to take a seat. "You got the look of a girl who don't know whether she's coming or going."

He sat down across the desk from me. "You ever play cards? 'Cause back home in Kentucky when we'd get too rowdy, my mom would get out the cards and get us playing poker or Hearts, just anything to make us sit down for a few minutes and relax."

I nodded. All at once my excitement had found a place to land. I took a deep breath to calm myself and tried to look innocent, like a girl who maybe played Old Maid or Crazy Eights from time to time.

"Well, then, reach into that top desk drawer and pull out a deck of cards. You know how to play gin rummy?"

I nodded again. "I think so," I said, sounding doubtful. As a matter of fact, the Colonel had taught me how to play gin when I was six and there was no one alive who could beat me two games in a row. But I kept a straight face as Private Hollister explained the rules to me, told me about runs and knocks and how to keep score.

Private Hollister leaned forward and picked up the cards. "I'll go ahead and deal first, just to get us started. You think you understand how to play?"

"I'm pretty sure," I said. "Just tell me if I mess up."

He smiled. Private Hollister had the face of a ten-year-old, about a thousand freckles across his nose, sticking-out ears, eyelashes like a girl's. It was hard to believe he was a grown man. But looking around at the soldiers playing pool and pinball, it was hard to believe any of them were full-fledged adults. They all looked like TJ, barely five minutes out of high school.

"So what's got you so full of beans today, anyway?" Private Hollister asked, shuffling the cards. "Or are you always this way and I just ain't noticed it yet?"

I swayed in my seat, the excitement rearing up in me again. "My brother just left for Vietnam. He's going to be a combat medic for the 51st Medical Company. He's the third generation in my family to join the Army. I'd join too, if they'd let me."

"How old are you, anyway? Eleven? You think they let many eleven-year-olds enlist?"

"I'll be thirteen in December," I told him, sitting up as straight as I could so maybe I would look old and mature. Not that I cared what people thought about my appearance. But even if I wasn't pretty in an obvious way, if my hair was just-barely-blond instead of a golden yellow, if my eyes were gray instead of blue, even if I was as scrawny as a bundle of twigs, there was no doubt in my mind I looked at least twelve and a half. "In fact," I said to Private Hollister, "my mom's due date was in November, only I came later than they thought I would. So I'm closer to thirteen than my birthday would have you believe."

"Oh. Well, you look eleven. I got a sister back home in Kentucky who's eleven, so that's how I know." Private Hollister began dealing. "You really a colonel's daughter?"

"Yep." I didn't want to sound snobbish about it, but I didn't want to sound so friendly that he thought it was okay to mistake me for an eleven-year-old.

"Full bird?"

I nodded.

"Man, oh man." Private Hollister shook his head. "I better not mess up around you. I might find myself in-country too."

"In what country?"

"Vietnam. That's what they call it when you're there. They say you're in-country. But me, I want to be way, way out of country, if you know what I mean."

I shook my head in sheer disbelief. "You're a soldier. You're supposed to fight."

Private Hollister put down the deck, picked

up his hand. "Maybe," he said. "But from what I've heard, I'd rather be here than there. No offense to your brother."

"Actually, he wasn't planning on going," I said, fanning out my cards to see what hand I'd been dealt. "He was supposed to go to college. But then he changed his mind. You want me to start?"

"Yeah, go ahead." Then Private Hollister cocked his head to one side and raised an eyebrow, like what I'd said just hit him. "Your brother could've gone to college, but he went to 'Nam instead?"

I discarded, picked up a card from the top of the deck. "I guess he got his priorities straight."

"Man, oh man, giving up college for a chance to dance with a Bouncing Betty. One of them things falls at your feet, whammo! It blows right up in your face." Private Hollister shook his head sorrowfully, discarded, drew a card.

I picked up his card, discarded, rapped my knuckles against the desktop. "Knock."

Private Hollister practically fell out of his chair. "You're knocking? How can you be knocking already?"

"Beginner's luck, I guess." I spread out my cards on the desk, a run of five, seven of diamonds through the jack, plus a pair of threes and a pair of queens.

"You scammed me!"

"I don't know what you're talking about. Just give me your cards and let me deal."

Then it was one hand after another, cards slapping, knuckles knocking, and me staying ahead the whole way through.

"All right," Private Hollister said when game thirty-seven was over. He looked at his watch. "I think I've gotten you calmed down enough. You ready to do a little work?"

"Combat ready," I told him.

Private Hollister laughed. "You're Army all the way, ain't you?"

"I'm Army through and through," I told him. "I mean it, if they'd let me go to Vietnam tomorrow, I'd go. I could be an ambulance driver or something like that."

"You even know how to drive a car?"

"Of course I know how to drive a car," I lied.

"I've been driving since I was eight. We were stationed in Germany then, and in Germany they let anybody drive who can see over a steering wheel."

Private Hollister stood up. "Now I know you're lying. You gotta be eighteen to drive over there. That's a fact."

I shrugged. "Must be a new law."

"Well, *you* might want to go to Vietnam, and you might be happy about your brother going to Vietnam," Private Hollister said, walking to the supply closet. "But I know your mom ain't happy about it."

"My mother is an Army mom," I said. I took the broom he handed me from the closet. "She knows that wars have to be fought and we need soldiers to fight them."

"What you're talking about is philosophy," Private Hollister said. "I'm talking about feelings. Ain't no mother happy about her son going to war."

"She'll be happy when we win," I told him.

Private Hollister looked skeptical. "If you say so."

"I don't just say so. I know so."

And I did know so. I knew it like I knew my name:

Jamie Dexter. I knew it like I knew my birthday: December 10. I knew it like I knew the flag: fifty stars, thirteen stripes, red, white, and blue, all in all a piece of cloth worth going to war for.

I was six months away from turning thirteen and I thought I knew everything.

two

We were stationed at Fort Hood, Texas, a flat piece of real estate that threatened to burst into flames every afternoon from June through September. The Colonel was the chief of staff, which meant for all intents and purposes he ran the show.

The Colonel was born to run the show, and he had a drawer full of medals and ribbons to prove it. One of his medals was for saving another soldier's life out in the field. I used to sneak it from his top dresser drawer and turn it over in my hands, feeling the power of it like an electric pulse running up and down my fingers.

It had always been my dream to shine in the

Colonel's eyes as brightly as one of those medals. My brother, TJ, had no problem in that regard. He was a varsity running back three years straight, made every football team he'd ever tried out for. The Colonel loved football. It was number three on his list of most loved things. Number one was everybody in our family—my mother, TJ, and me, in that order—number two was the United States Army, and number three, hands down, no questions asked, was football. College football, professional football, a game of touch football in the backyard, it did not matter to the Colonel.

More than once the Colonel had told me that if I had been a boy, I would have been a star football player on any team you'd care to name. Well, maybe he didn't say it in those words, but that's what he meant every time he yelled, "Look at her arm! Watch that girl throw a spiral pass! You can't buy talent like that, no sir!" Some nights after dinner, we'd throw the ball around, the Colonel still wearing his uniform, his everyday battle fatigues and shiny lace-up combat boots that didn't seem to slow him down a bit for all their heaviness.

He'd toss me the football, turn and pound across the backyard grass, and I'd cock my arm back for the pass, then let the ball fly. It would spiral smoothly through the air for a few seconds before the Colonel pulled it down with one hand, no problem, and tucked it under his arm.

"Pathfinders!" he'd yell, zigzagging across the yard toward the imaginary end zone.

"Combat ready, sir!" I'd yell back, completing the old 8th Infantry Division call-and-response we'd learned as kids, which was part of our life, just like answering the phone "Colonel Dexter's quarters" or making sure we had our military IDs with us whenever we went to the PX or the commissary so we could prove who we were, proud citizens of the United States Army. *Hooah*, as we liked to say. *Hooah*, yes sir.

Even more than football, the Colonel loved the Army. He loved starched and stiff uniforms and boots polished to a high shine. He was crazy about military parades and had dragged me and TJ to parade grounds from Fort Benning to Fort Ord. I'd even seen him get teary-eyed when the troops passing in front of the inspection stand turned right-face to salute whatever bigwig officer was sitting in the catbird seat. It got to him every time.

"The Army way is the right way," he'd say to us whenever we piled into our blue Ford station wagon to start out for a new destination—Fort Hood, Fort Campbell, Fort Leavenworth. It was the pep talk he gave us in case we were feeling sad about moving again. "It's about duty, it's about honor, it's about sacrifice."

If you weren't an Army brat, that kind of talk would probably have you rolling your eyes. But we believed it. I believed it. It made me proud to hear the Colonel say it. When he'd saved that soldier's life out in the field, in the middle of combat exercises with artillery and tanks, he'd risked his own life, came a hair's width away from getting killed. Sometimes at night in bed I'd get cold and still all over thinking about that, how the Colonel might be dead right now. But in the daylight I wore his bravery like a badge of honor.

TJ and I loved the Army so much we'd spent most of our time as kids playing Army with our friends, planning out battles and strategies in deep, serious voices, setting up hundreds of little green Army guys out under the trees. I always played TJ's second in command, moving the green men around as he ordered, gathering sticks and acorns and whatever else he thought we might need in the heat of combat.

One time, after a fierce battle against Bobby and Charles Kerner, whose troops stubbornly refused to surrender for almost two hours, TJ unwrapped a piece of gum he'd had in his jeans pocket and folded up the foil wrapper into a shiny triangle. He chewed the gum for a minute, then stuck it to the foil triangle and stuck the triangle to my T-shirt.

"What did you do that for?" I asked him, feeling the wet gob of gum through the fabric of my shirt.

"It's a medal," TJ explained. "For courage under fire."

I wore that medal for two weeks, until the gum finally lost its stick somewhere between the school playground and my second-grade classroom.

The Colonel had been an Army brat too, and

he loved telling the story of how the Army had lifted his father up from poverty to a good life. Papa Joe had been the fastest boy in his school, even with his shoes flopping apart, and one day he'd been spotted by an Army recruiter, who told him he ought to sign up for the service the minute he turned eighteen. So that's just what Papa Joe did. With his first paycheck he bought his mother a new dress, the first store-bought dress she'd ever had.

Every once in a while the Colonel pulled out the box of things he'd saved growing up, when he had traveled all over the place just like we did, from this post to that one. He showed us ticket stubs from train trips through Germany and Italy, and matchbooks he'd collected from restaurants in just about every American city you could think of.

"Kids," he'd say, leaning back on the couch, his arms spread out wide, "I am a man of the world, full of knowledge and vision, a lover of international cuisine, an appreciator of fine art and good-looking women, and I have the United States Army to thank for this most excellent state of affairs."

"Oh, Tom," my mother would say, laughing, the music of it all high and bubbly. Then she'd roll her eyes, acting as though she were immune to the Colonel's charms. "What you are is a man who likes the sound of his own voice."

"You love me, woman," the Colonel would bellow. "Don't be afraid to admit it." And then he'd turn to me and TJ and say, "All the ladies love me. They can't help it," and we'd blush and giggle, and I'd think that nobody in the world had a father as outstanding as the Colonel. I loved the Army, too, for making him exactly the way he was.

You would have thought the very *idea* of TJ enlisting would have sent the Colonel cartwheeling down Tank Destroyer Boulevard, Fort Hood's main drag. But when the announcement came, over a Sunday dinner in March, a couple of days after TJ's eighteenth birthday, he didn't say a word for a long time, just looked down at his plate like the medium-rare steak staring back up at him was about to whisper the meaning of life.

"Aren't you going to say anything, sir?" TJ finally asked, when the Colonel's silence was starting to make us all feel nervous. It wasn't like him to shut up for any length of time.

After another minute, the Colonel sighed. He's a big man, six foot four standing around in his socks, a once-upon-a-time West Point defensive tackle, a regular bruiser, so it was funny to hear him sigh like a Sunday school teacher. He began tapping his finger against the table like he was keeping time to a song playing inside his head.

"The point is, son, you're going to college in six months." He tapped slowly at first, then worked up to rat-a-tat-tat speed. "The University of Georgia, class of 1973. Then medical school. You want to enlist after that, I'll hand you the pen myself."

TJ sawed at his T-bone in his slow, deliberate way. "College is the coward's way out, sir. How can I go to college when guys I played football with are fighting in Vietnam? Eddie McNeil's missing in action."

The Colonel took a deep breath before he spoke again. I wondered if he was thinking about Eddie, who had been one of TJ's best friends when TJ was a junior and Eddie was a senior and could do no wrong on the football field or any other place he decided to show up. He went straight from his graduation gown into an Army uniform, and a few months later shipped out to Vietnam. Two weeks ago, the day after Valentine's Day, the principal had announced over the loudspeaker that Eddie was MIA. TJ had been pale as a ghost when I saw him get off the bus that afternoon, and when he told me why, I'd wanted to say something to him, but I didn't know what to say except, "He's probably okay."

TJ didn't say anything in reply. He just walked inside the house and closed the door to his room behind him.

"You won't find Eddie when you go over there, son," the Colonel finally said. "You can't put yourself on a one-man mission to go find your friend in the jungle."

I eyeballed TJ, trying to figure out if Eddie McNeil was his real reason for enlisting, or if he was looking for any reason to go. We'd been playing war all our lives, and more than once TJ had said he'd like to get a taste of real combat, to see if he could handle it. Sometime around tenth grade, when it became clear TJ was talented at science, the Colonel started pushing medical school on him, and slowly TJ had come around to the Colonel's point of view, but I would have bet money that part of him still wanted to test his mettle in battle.

Now TJ said, "I want to go to Vietnam because it's the right thing to do, sir. That's the only reason. I'll go to college when I get back."

Up to this point, my mother had not said a word. This was her way. She liked to let everyone else talk first, to get what they had up their craw out of their system before she weighed in. But now she leaned forward, her eyes rimmed in red, and said, "If you want to be a hero, then go to medical school. You can save hundreds of lives when the time comes."

"I've already signed the papers," TJ said. He tapped lightly against his salad plate with his fork, like he was underlining his point. "I'm going to join the Medical Corps. It'll be good experience."

"You've got time to change your mind, son,"

the Colonel said. "It says so right there in the fine print."

TJ stared him down. "Do you really expect me to do that, sir?"

"We'll talk about it in a few days," the Colonel said, cutting into his steak. "When you've had more time to think about what you've done."

"You should go, TJ." I leaned over and grabbed his wrist, like I'd pull him all the way over there myself if I had to. "I'd go to Vietnam in a minute if they let me. Besides, you don't know when we'll get another war."

"Oh, honey," my mother said. "You don't know anything about war. You're just a little girl."

"I'm starting eighth grade in September, which is hardly a little girl, and I read *Time* magazine," I argued. "I know plenty about war." S468130

"That's enough, Jamie," the Colonel said. But I thought deep down he had to be proud of me, and of TJ, too. He'd raised us, after all. He'd raised us to believe in the Army way. And as far as I was concerned, he'd raised us right.

three

Once we started playing cards together, Private Hollister and I fit right in with each other. If one of us had been a lot better than the other, we probably wouldn't have become friends. But we were evenly matched, and even better than that, we both were good. It made us admire one another. It made us easy with each other.

"How many brothers and sisters do you have?" I asked one morning as Private Hollister was dealing cards for a game of rummy. We didn't know it yet, but this would become our game for the summer. Once we got started playing gin, it never occurred to us to play anything else.

"Seven. All of us *B*s, too," he said, flipping the cards into neat piles.

"You're bees?"

"Like the letter *B*," he explained. "Bucky, Brenda, Betsy, Burl, Barney, Barbara, Bitsy, and Bob."

"You've got a Bitsy *and* a Betsy?"

"Something wrong with that?"

I picked up my cards and started sorting them out. "No, it just seems like it could get confusing, having two people with names that are so close together."

"Nah," Private Hollister said, fanning out his cards and studying them. "Bitsy's about six foot tall, and Betsy's a tiny thing. You could never mistake them for one another."

I couldn't believe how bad my hand was. The closest I had to anything was a pair of twos. No runs, no three-of-a-kinds. It was all deadwood. I needed to make some good draws and fast. I leaned forward and took a card from the top of the deck. "So who's your parents' favorite out of all the kids?" I asked, happy to see that I'd picked up the two of clubs. I discarded an ace.

"My dad don't have a favorite," Private Hollister said, picking up my discard. "He's pretty much lost interest in all of us. But I'm my mom's favorite, no doubt about it. Who do you think taught me how to play cards? It's because I stayed home all the time from school, acting like I was sick. I didn't much like school."

"Why not?"

Private Hollister discarded. "Because school didn't much like me. Mom taught me cards when I stayed home, and I got so good she didn't mind me skipping."

"My brother's always been the Colonel's favorite," I said. "But it's not like the Colonel doesn't like me, too. He does. He and TJ just have a special bond together."

"That's how it is with fathers and sons," Private Hollister said. "Well, not with me and my dad, but I've seen it in a lot of other families. Usually it has to do with sports."

I nodded. "Football. Even though I like football too."

"Yeah, but you're a girl. No father dreams of

seeing his daughter playing in the NFL. Maybe you should try out for cheerleading."

I put down my cards. "Do I look like the cheerleading type to you?"

Private Hollister studied me for a minute. "You might not be peppy enough, that's true. But you'll be cute in a couple of years. I can tell. Bitsy was plain as day until she was fourteen, and then, look out, buddy. That girl blossomed like a sunflower."

"Hell's bells," I said. "I don't want to be a stupid cheerleader."

"You know, I think it's against the rules to cuss in here," Private Hollister said. He checked his cards again, then knocked, signaling that he was ready to count points. "Anyway, you're too young to cuss."

"I'll be thirteen in December," I told him for what had to have been the hundredth time that week. "Thirteen is old enough for cussing. So's twelve, for that matter."

"For boys, maybe. Not for girls. Girls ain't supposed to cuss at all."

"That's a stupid rule. Either everybody cusses or nobody cusses."

"Well, no cussing when we've got customers. That's a fair rule."

"I suppose."

I laid down my hand and counted the points from my unmatched cards. I'd managed to come back from a lousy deal, but that wasn't enough to beat Private Hollister.

"Let's keep track of our games, you want to?" Private Hollister asked. He pulled a pen from his uniform pocket. "That's what me and Mom do at home. Just so you know who has bragging rights at the end of the day." Then he looked at me and grinned. "You know, I think you're working out here all right. I wasn't so sure you would at first."

"What do you mean, you didn't think I'd work out?" I asked, indignant.

Private Hollister took a second to write down our scores. "Well, (a) for one thing, you're a girl, and a lot of girls couldn't handle being around GIs all the time without getting all silly and giggly and just acting dumb about it. Turned out you're not that way, but I didn't know it at the time. And (b) you seemed kind of young. I think it's because you're short or something. Or maybe it was the way you were dressed. Of course, that was before I knew you were a card shark."

My first day of work I'd shown up in a white blouse, a pair of pressed Bermuda shorts, and penny loafers, no socks. It wasn't the first time I'd been to the rec center, but it was the neatest I'd ever dressed for a visit. On gray winter Sunday afternoons, the Colonel, TJ, and I would play pool on the pockmarked, cigarette-scarred green tables, and I'd wear a sweatshirt and old jeans, happy to be shed of my church clothes for the day. The Colonel was an excellent pool player, and he was teaching me and TJ all his tricks. My mother did not like this one bit. She thought it was inappropriate for a girl my age, on the very edge of womanhood, to play pool and spend Sunday afternoons in a smoke-filled room alongside young soldiers who were not above using colorful language if the situation called for it.

The Colonel, on the other hand, thought any girl worth her salt should be able to shoot a game of eightball. So when he told me midsummer that if I didn't get over the fact that my two best friends had moved away within two weeks of each other, both of their families reassigned overseas, and if I didn't quit moping around on the living-room couch eating Snickers bars and reading old comic books, he'd get me a job peeling tomatoes at the mess hall, I suggested that I could volunteer at the rec center instead. I told him it would give me the opportunity to serve soldiers, which I knew he'd like, since one of his favorite sayings was, "Service to others is the highest calling."

I'd never been to the rec center on a weekday morning, and I'd been surprised when no crack of pool balls or ringing pinball machines greeted me my first day of work. The only sound in the whole place was the insect-whir of a ceiling fan and the soft flipping of pages. A soldier sat slouched behind the checkout desk, his face hidden behind a Superman comic book. When he looked up and saw me, he shoved the comic book into a drawer and came to attention.

"I'm the new volunteer," I said, hoping the tone of my voice would let him know that comic book reading was fine by me, although I was not a DC

Comics fan myself, preferring the Marvel heroes as a general rule. "Are you the person I need to talk to?"

He reddened a little and stood. "Private Hollister, miss," he said. "Private First Class Bucky Hollister. My CO told me what your name was, but now I don't rightly remember."

I stuck out my hand. "Jamie Dexter. I'm very excited to be working here."

Private Hollister looked at my hand as though I'd just offered him a live trout to do the tango with. His face got even redder, and so did his ears, which stuck out about a mile in either direction. He couldn't have been a day over nineteen.

"Well, if you want to know the truth," he said, backing away a few steps, like he was going to do whatever it took to avoid shaking hands with me, "there's not a whole lot to do here in the mornings. Most guys don't show up until lunchtime."

"Maybe you should serve doughnuts in the morning," I said, an idea that appealed to me as soon as I came up with it. "People will show up early if there are doughnuts around."

"I don't know about that, miss," Private Hollister said. "I'd have to check with my CO."

After we'd been playing cards together a week or so, Private Hollister admitted he never checked anything with his CO. "But if you're still looking for a project, I thought of something you could do," he said to me after he'd written down the scores for our final hand in his notebook. "You know anything about developing film?"

"Not really," I told him. "TJ's the photographer in our family. He took pictures for the school paper when it wasn't football season. He printed all the pictures himself."

In fact, most of TJ's allowance and his tips from bagging groceries at the commissary went to film, camera equipment, and photography magazines. Most of my allowance went to Archie comics, Snickers bars, and overdue library book fines.

"You interested in learning something? Because I've got all these guys who come in here with questions about how to develop their film in the darkroom back there," Private Hollister said, nodding toward the hallway that led to the rec center's arts and crafts area. "Personally, I don't know a thing about it. Might be good if somebody who worked here did."

"I'd rather play cards," I told him. "I'm not really all that interested in photography."

But then I got TJ's first package, and suddenly I was very interested.

four

TJ's first letter to me wasn't a letter at all. It was a roll of film.

The package was waiting on the front hall table when I got home from the rec center on a Friday afternoon. I rushed to tear it open, but my mother stepped in between me and the mail.

"Let's wait until your father gets home, honey," she said, picking up the package and holding it out of reach. "TJ's first letter from Vietnam is a special occasion."

I paced around the house for the rest of the afternoon, wanting so bad to get my hand on TJ's letter. TJ's package. Well, maybe not a big package.

Maybe it was more like a padded envelope. But something was in there. Something from the war. Every five minutes I'd call out to my mother, "The Colonel won't mind if we open it. He's not sentimental about things like letters."

"Oh, you'd be surprised by how sentimental your father is. He's an old softy," my mother would call back.

I harrumphed at that. The Colonel was as soft as a granite wall.

But I have to admit he seemed almost emotional when he saw TJ's package on the table. "Why don't we take a look at this thing," he said, and I could tell he was as eager as I was to see what was inside. Normally the Colonel hardly even said hello when he walked in the door after work. He liked to go upstairs and change, first thing.

The three of us sat down on the living room couch, and the Colonel used his penknife to open the padded envelope. He shook it a bit, and a black film canister dropped out. The Colonel examined it, and handed it to me. There was a note attached. "'Jamie: No facilities here,'" I read.

"'Please develop and send contact sheets.'"

No signature. No message about where he was or what war was like. Just a roll of film. And what did he mean *Send contact sheets*? You didn't get contact sheets when the PX developed your film. All you got were pictures and negatives. One reason TJ said he learned to develop his own film is that he liked having all of his pictures printed on one sheet of paper, to see which ones were worth blowing up to eight by ten. Why hadn't he written *Please have developed at PX*? He knew I didn't have the faintest idea about how to develop film.

But I'd known TJ long enough to know this about him: When it came to photography, he did not make casual mistakes. If he'd wanted me to take it to the PX, he would have written, *Take it to the PX*. In fact, if he'd wanted it taken to the PX, he would have just mailed it to my mother.

But he hadn't. He'd sent my mother and the Colonel a boring letter about the flight over and mess-hall food. "'Everything comes out of a tin can,'" the Colonel read. "'Even the meat. Even the chocolate cream pie. One guy I know actually wrote his mom asking her to send fresh tomatoes. I'd like to see that box when he opens it.'"

The Colonel and my mother laughed, like that was some great joke. Personally I couldn't care less that he'd made friends with a guy all the way from Alaska or that he'd seen a cockroach bigger than his fist on his first night in-country, information also included in the letter. What did that have to do with anything important?

He'd sent me the roll of film with the instructions to develop it. And the more I thought about it, the more I felt like that was fine by me. No one else was going to see TJ's war pictures before I saw them. Maybe I hadn't gotten a bona fide letter, but the pictures were my property.

"You know who can help me with this?" I asked Private Hollister the next day, showing him the film. "I mean, how do you even get the film out?"

"I told you, nobody around here really knows." Private Hollister was wrapping tape around a Ping-Pong paddle handle as he spoke, cussing under his breath when he wrapped his fingers, too. Overall, the job appeared to be slow going. "I mean, there are a few guys who come in and use the darkroom, but it's hard to say when they'll show up. This one guy? Brezinski? All he takes pictures of are tanks. And there's Sergeant Byrd, he comes in a lot in the afternoon. He's a strange dude, though."

"What's so strange about him?"

"I heard he was at Khe Sanh with 1st Cav, and that it did something to him. I see him around, and once in a while he's friendly, but mostly he's just up in his own head. He goes off post with a camera by himself whenever he's off duty. You almost always see him with a camera."

"What's Khe Sanh?" I asked, hopping up to take a seat on a pool table, a practice strictly forbidden when anyone was in the main room, but one that Private Hollister let me get away with if no one else was there.

"It's a Marine base, only Army units are there too. It's a real bad spot, way out in the boonies. They say you're lucky if you don't get shot just getting on or off the plane at the landing strip. That's happened to plenty of guys. Guys who were done with their tours and heading out to go back to the States."

"You think he'd teach me to develop film?"

Private Hollister peeled a strip of tape from his hand. "I guess so. He's strange, but he seems nice enough. Usually you see him here around three."

I was waiting in the darkroom at two forty-five, clutching TJ's film cartridge in my hand. Butterflies whirred in my stomach as I imagined accidentally exposing the film to the light or dropping it into a sink of developing solution and not being able to get it out. I was dying to know what the war was like. TJ's letter to my parents hadn't said much at all, just that he was adjusting, that he liked the guys in his unit, that he hadn't had to work in a combat situation yet. There was nothing in it that let you taste the true flavor of war, smell the smoke of bombs, hear the helicopters as they took off from the middle of the jungle.

"I think you're asking a lot of TJ, Sport," the Colonel said to me when I complained about his lackluster letter. "He's been over there two weeks. He hasn't had time to wipe his rear end yet, much less write us a poem about the joys of Southeast Asia."

"You think he likes it over there?" I asked. We were eating dinner, my mother's famous squash casserole, the Colonel's favorite, and I could tell I was wearing him thin with my comments and questions. The Colonel liked to be able to savor his food, especially when it came to cheesy casseroles covered with buttered breadcrumbs toasted to a golden brown.

"I think he probably hates it," the Colonel replied, his fork halfway to his mouth, strings of cheese stretching to his plate. "I think he's probably thinking about this squash casserole right now and remembering how soft his pillow upstairs is."

"I think you're wrong," I said, and felt even more determined to learn how to develop TJ's film. Then the true story would come out, with TJ at the center of it, the hero of it all.

"Hollister said you were looking for me?"

The GI who entered the room most closely resembled a whooping crane, or at least what I imagined a whooping crane to look like, tall and thin to the point of distraction, a pointy nose, the sort of person who didn't quite seem comfortable in his skin but might surprise you by being an amazing dancer.

"Are you Sgt. Byrd?"

"Ah-yup. In the flesh. The one and only. That's Byrd with a *Y*, by the way. I can't fly, but I won't crap on your windshield, either."

Well, what are you supposed to say to that? I pointed to the name strip sewn over the pocket of his flak jacket. It read BYRD, T. "What's the *T* stand for?"

"Theophilus. Middle name of James. You can call me Ted, if you want to be informal about it. I'll call you ma'am, unless you have another moniker you'd prefer to be referred by."

"Jamie's fine," I told him. "You think you could teach me how to develop this roll of film?" I held it up. "My brother sent it to me from Vietnam."

Sgt. Byrd eyed the film with interest. "Where's he at?"

"He's with the 51st Medical Company in Phu Bai," I told him. "He's a medic."

"Hard job. No gun, no glory. A lot of bullet-dodging. Medics are the true war heroes, if you want my opinion."

That's when I decided I liked Sgt. Byrd.

He set down the camera bag he was carrying and motioned me to toss him the film cartridge. "Good film, medium speed, which is right for the kind of photography I bet he's doing," he said, examining it. "And black-and-white, which makes our job a lot easier. Color processing is a headache. It's better just to send color film to a lab."

He picked up a large white plastic spool from the counter. "You ever see one of these things? It's called a film reel. The hardest part of the job. You've got to get the film from the cartridge onto this baby, and you've got to do it blind." He pointed to a door on the other side of the room. "You sit in that little closet over there and make it happen."

"In the dark? What if I ruin the film before it's even developed?"

Sgt. Byrd reached into his bag and pulled out another film cartridge, which he handed to me.

"You can practice on this one. I'll shout directions to you through the door."

"I don't want to ruin your film," I protested.

"Ain't nothing but a thing, my young friend," said Sgt. Byrd. "I'm all about the process. The end product is less important to me. You ruin some film, big deal. I'll take more pictures."

I took the film, the film reel, a canister, and canister cover into the closet and closed the door. I was in complete darkness. "Okay, what do I do first?" I asked, fumbling around, trying to feel what was the reel, what was the canister, holding on to the film cartridge for dear life.

He walked me through the process: I unwound the film from its spool and slid one end of it into a slot on the outer edge of the reel. The tricky part was loading the film onto the reel, which meant catching the edges of the film on the reel's teeth. This took me about twenty tries and a lot of hot-blooded cussing to accomplish. Once I finally got the film loaded, all I had to do was insert the reel in the canister and cover it. That part was a cinch.

"I think I'm ready to open the door now," I told Sgt. Byrd.

"Is the canister lid on tightly?"

"I think so."

"Then emerge and let's see how you did."

Sgt. Byrd was full of high praise for my work. "I've never seen anyone figure out how to load a film reel that fast," he told me. "You're a natural, kid."

I felt the heat rise to my cheeks. I'd never been called a natural at anything before. I was good at several things: throwing a football, unknotting knots, multiplying fractions. I could draw hands that almost looked real, except the thumbs were never 100 percent right. But no one had ever noticed a pure, natural-born talent in me before now.

"You ready to try your brother's film?"

I nodded. "Combat ready."

A shadow seemed to pass over Sgt. Byrd's face. "Let's call this a combat-free zone, how 'bout it? Combat-free, duty-free, fancy-free. Land of the free, home of the brave." He smiled and handed me TJ's film. "Time to get to work, what do you say, pal?"

"Okay," I told him. "I think I can do it."

He patted me on the shoulder. "Oh, you can do it all right. Like I said, you're a natural."

He was right. I was.

five

TJ started taking pictures in junior high school, when we were stationed on an Army post in Bad Kreuznach, a small German town an hour or so from Frankfurt. When you're an Army brat stationed in Germany, you're in for serious sight-seeing duty. You'll be dragged from castles to river cruises to medieval cities that are damp and cold even in the heart of summer. Your parents will feel it is their solemn obligation to drag you to these places over and over, whenever relatives come visit, whenever it's a bright and shiny Saturday and there's no football to be played, whenever you complain because the TV stateside is so much better than the lousy Armed Forces Network.

There are a couple of ways of dealing with your life as a constant tourist. If you're like me, you'll develop a serious comic book habit and never leave home without at least five Archies, three Beetle Baileys, and a Little Lulu or two tucked into your backpack. You'll learn how to read comic books while you're walking, and how to shove them into the back of your jeans the second your parents turn around to see why you're moving so slow.

If you're like TJ, you'll learn how to use a camera.

Taking pictures was about the first thing TJ ever did that made him different from the Colonel. The Colonel was the gung-ho type, always in forward motion. But to take pictures, you have to stop, step back, look around. Taking pictures, TJ stood still for once in his life. Up until the time he picked up his first camera, he matched the Colonel stride for stride, no matter where we were. If we were home, you could find the two of them either playing football or working in the yard, also known as the Colonel's domestic domain, digging, watering, weeding, putting pesticide powder on the rose bushes. If we were at the PX or commissary, TJ and the Colonel went into competition mode, seeing who could find the most items on the shopping list the fastest.

But the camera slowed TJ down. I think that's why the Colonel never made a big to-do about TJ's pictures the way everybody else did. And TJ's pictures were great. Even I could see what my mother was always saying: TJ had a good eye. You'd look at pictures he'd taken of an old stone wall circling round some ancient city, and you'd see things you hadn't when you were standing right in front of it. You'd see the images the shadowy parts of the stones made, or the little piece of graffiti someone had drawn where the wall met the ground.

The Colonel didn't see the point of it. "You can live your life or you can watch it," he'd say every time one of our expeditions got slowed down because TJ wanted to take a picture of something, a statue, a duck waddling down the middle of the road, a little kid who'd just dropped his ice-cream cone on his lap. "But if you're going to watch, stand back, because those of us who choose to live are going to run you down."

"Just because you never learned how to focus a camera doesn't mean you have to pick on TJ," my mother would chide him. The Colonel always laughed when she said that, but you could tell TJ's photography still got on his nerves somehow.

For years TJ took his film to the PX to be developed. But when we moved to Fort Hood his junior year, he signed up for a photography elective and learned how to develop his film himself. For the most part, his pictures were still a sightseer's pictures: Here's this interesting building, here's this weird-looking tree, over there, see that 1958 Coupe DeVille?

But after TJ enlisted, his pictures changed. One, he started taking pictures of people. Two, he started taking pictures of the moon.

"Do you really think the moon is all that interesting?" I asked him one afternoon when we were sitting in the kitchen after school, not long after TJ had enlisted, his latest pictures spread out all over the table. In some of them, the moon was just a bright blob of light in the night sky. In others, it was thin and sharp-edged as a dime. "A comet would be interesting, and a meteor plummeting toward Earth would be very interesting. But the moon just kind of sits there all night."

"It's got shadows in it," TJ explained. "From the craters. I think the shadows are interesting. And I like the idea that now there are human footprints on the moon's surface. There's something pretty cool about that. And, I don't know, it's this place in space that people have actually gone to. Can you imagine flying through space to the moon?"

"You ever want to be an astronaut?" I traced a full moon in one of TJ's pictures, imagining I could see Neil Armstrong's footprints on its surface.

He shook his head. "Don't have the brains for it."

"You've got to be pretty smart to be a doctor."

"I'm doctor-smart, but not astronaut-smart."

"Well, now that you're joining the Army, maybe you'll stay in. You could be a general. I bet you're general-smart."

TJ grinned. "Maybe. Let's see if I'm smart enough to stay alive first."

——

"If you're going to be a medic, you won't be in any big battles." I didn't know whether to feel relieved or disappointed about this fact.

"Are you kidding? Who do you think is out there picking up the wounded? If you want to know the truth, I'd rather have gone Field Artillery. But I thought Mom would swallow the Medical Corps easier."

I looked at TJ with greater appreciation. Field Artillery. Now that was some serious business. Those were the guys with the mortars and the howitzers.

My favorite pictures of TJ's were of the track team. He photographed the races for the school paper, but the really good pictures were the ones of people right after they'd finished running. He'd get right up in their faces, and if you didn't know they were runners you'd think they were witnessing momentous events, their faces were so joyful or full of pain, the sweat glistening like tears on their cheeks. I didn't know much about art, but I knew those pictures were beautiful.

"You go to college, you'll have access to some

great darkroom equipment on campus, I'd bet," the Colonel said one night after dinner. It was during that period where TJ still had time to walk away from his enlistment contract, and the Colonel couldn't keep himself from nudging TJ in that direction. I was pretty sure my mother was putting him up to it.

We were out in the backyard, working in the garden. TJ leaned against the hoe he'd been turning over dirt with and said, "I'll take my cameras with me to Vietnam. I bet I'll get some great pictures there."

"Did it ever occur to you that you might not get sent to Vietnam?" the Colonel asked. He smiled. You could tell this idea had just come to him, and it had cheered him right up. "They need medics in all kinds of places. You might get stuck in the desert around Fort Huachuca. They might need you at Fort Dix, in New Jersey. You want to give up college for a trip to New Jersey?"

"They're sending everyone to Vietnam these days, sir," I informed the Colonel, not so much to argue with him, but to show him I was a well-read individual. "It was in *Time* magazine. They're going to draft a quarter-million men to send over there this year."

"*Time* magazine doesn't know everything there is to know about what the Army does," the Colonel grumbled. He dropped the subject and returned to his tomato plants, which were just beginning to shoot up out of the dirt.

But TJ didn't want to drop the subject. "I'll be able to take some amazing pictures over there," he said, sounding suddenly excited by the prospect. "How far south is Vietnam, anyway? It's not in the Southern Hemisphere, is it? The sky would be completely different if it was."

He went inside to look up "Vietnam" in the encyclopedia. And that's when I wondered if half the reason he enlisted was for the adventure of it. To take pictures of things he'd never seen before. He might never make it to the moon, but he could get an all-expenses-paid trip to Southeast Asia.

The Colonel shook his head. "He thinks he's going on safari with a telephoto lens. He thinks he's going to have a spare second over there to take pictures. Like hell he will. He'll be too busy trying not to get himself killed."

But the Colonel was wrong about that.

He was wrong about a lot, it turned out.

six

I only had one friend who had a brother in Vietnam.
So when I'd finished developing and printing TJ's
film, which took me two days in the darkroom, Sgt.
Byrd walking me through the process step by step,
I took the photographs to Cindy Lorenzo's house,
even though I knew there was only a slight chance
she'd appreciate them. Cindy was not actually my
first choice for an audience, but since my two best
friends, Liz and Pam, had moved away, and my
next best friend, Jennifer, was spending the summer with her grandmother, I didn't have much of
a pool to pick from.

There were good things and bad things about

being friends with Cindy Lorenzo. The worst thing was that she was an eleven-year-old girl whose brain was still on the first-grade level. She could read and dress herself and ride her fancy bicycle in wobbly circles around her front yard, but she couldn't think straight at all. It was like her emotions got in the way of her thoughts. She was nervous and excitable and shaky around the edges. She hit and bit.

The good things about being friends with Cindy Lorenzo included the fact that I could tell her my secrets and she never blabbed a word of what I said. I could brag on myself, and she wouldn't raise her eyebrows every few seconds the way regular people would to keep me from getting too puffed up with my own greatness. Some days Cindy acted like she thought I was some sort of hero, and that's a feeling that's hard to resist, no matter who's having it about you.

"I'm not a ballerina, but I could be one if I wanted to," Cindy informed me the minute I walked into the Lorenzos' front hallway. "Joey said I couldn't ever be a ballerina, so I kicked him."

Joey was one of Cindy's invisible friends. Most little kids had invisible friends who were nice and friendly, but with Cindy's crowd it was hit-or-miss. She complained all the time about her invisible friend Suzanne, who was a pincher. "I just stuck my tongue out at her, that's what I did," she'd say, to let me know that Suzanne's pinching had not gone unavenged.

"Bless your heart, Jamie, you don't have a bit of tan this summer. You need to get yourself over to the swimming pool." Mrs. Lorenzo swooped into the room in a cloud of rosy perfume. It was hard to make your eyes go from Mrs. Lorenzo to Cindy and back again and convince yourself they were related. Cindy was tall for her age, but she walked hunched over like an old lady, and her skin was splotchy and drab. Mrs. Lorenzo, on the other hand, fluttered and flittered hither and yon, high color on her cheeks, her hair piled on top of her head in one dramatic style or another. She and my mother were best friends, which is why Cindy and I got thrown together so much. That, and the fact that the Lorenzos lived across the street from us, and

I could babysit Cindy when her parents wanted to go out to dinner.

"Let's go talk to Brutus," Cindy said, tugging on my hand. "He says he misses you, even if he likes it better over here with me."

I followed her upstairs to her bedroom, looking as I always did at the family pictures that lined the wall above the railing. There were Cindy's brothers, both grown, the older one, Nathan, even married with a baby. You could see that they were Mrs. Lorenzo's children, no questions asked, with their handsome faces and pretty brown eyes.

The picture that fascinated me the most was the one at the very top of the stairs, the family picture the Lorenzos had taken the year before, when both sons came over to visit at the same time, right before Mark, who was twenty-three, left for Vietnam. It was a "Who in this picture doesn't belong?" picture, with the answer being Cindy. The other four Lorenzos were looking the photographer straight in the eye, their white teeth gleaming, dark hair shining, everything pressed and straight and starched, Col. Lorenzo and Mark both in uniform. Cindy sat slouched next to her mother, her nervous eyes wandering away from the camera, her shoulders slumped in their little-old-lady slouch. It was like someone had snuck her into the picture as a joke, and the other Lorenzos were ignoring her the best they could.

"Brutus says he comes from Africa, but he never told you that because you don't like Africa," Cindy said, leading me into her room.

"I like Africa," I protested before I could remember not to get caught up in conversation with Cindy like she was just another one of my friends. Within seconds, I'd be arguing on her level, saying hurtful things just to feel superior.

"Brutus says you don't." Cindy reached over and pinched me. "So don't lie."

"Sorry." I rubbed the red welt on my arm. "I won't anymore."

Cindy sat primly on her neatly made bed, the pink chenille spread pulled tight, and reached across a pile of stuffed animals toward a raggedy, stretched-out boxer dog with fluff coming out of his left eye socket where the eye used to be. This was my beloved Brutus, given to me by TJ on my third birthday. According to my mother, he'd struggled hard over whether or not to give me Brutus or keep him for himself, but in the end brotherly love had won out. He'd named Brutus before he gave him to me, saying that if he ever got a dog, if our mom suddenly stopped being allergic to them, that's what he'd planned on calling it.

"You know you have to give Brutus back to me one day," I told Cindy, the way I did every time I came over. "I only loaned him to you. It's not for keeps."

Cindy hugged Brutus tight to her chest. "Brutus likes it here better, I told you he told me that. He told me that he hates you and wishes you would die."

You wouldn't think that some crazy thing Cindy Lorenzo said to you, something made up in her halfway working mind, could hurt your feelings, but Cindy's words could pinch as hard as her fingers. I knew I should just ignore her, and sometimes I could. But right then I wanted to pinch Cindy back.

"Hey, Cindy, do you want to go to the playground and see who's there? We could swing on the swings."

Cindy went pale, the brown splotches on her skin standing out worse than ever. "No, no, no, no," she said, the last "no" scaling into a wail. "No, I will not, no, no."

She curled up into a ball on her bed, still clutching Brutus. I felt a tiny pang of regret, but more than that, I felt like I'd gotten Cindy back and she deserved it. It was not the nicest part of myself that felt that way. Sometimes I thought it was too bad that I'd figured out Cindy couldn't stand being around a lot of people at once. A nicer person than me would never have used this information against Cindy. I tried not to do it too much, but every once in a while I couldn't help myself.

"Okay, okay," I said after a minute. I sat down next to her on the bed. "That's not what I came over to ask you, anyway. I wanted to show you the pictures TJ sent me from Vietnam. Well, he didn't send me the pictures, actually. He sent the film. I developed it by myself."

"TJ's a meanie!" Cindy shrieked. "I hate him!"

Cindy was in love with my brother. Her love had shown itself in a parade of little-kid insults and pinches and kicks. It was like watching the Three Stooges, the kind of funny that makes you laugh and wince at the same time.

"I developed this film myself," I repeated, wanting Cindy to be impressed, even though I knew that she wouldn't be. She'd probably never given one thought in her life to how pictures got from the camera to a piece of paper. Still, I liked saying it. "Sgt. Byrd taught me how to print pictures this very afternoon. He said I'm a natural, from start to finish."

Learning to develop the film had been easier than I thought it would be. Sgt. Byrd talked me through the whole process, making me do everything myself, saying that's the only way I'd learn it. When I finally pulled out the long strip of negatives from the processing tank, I felt like some kind of genius. I hung the negatives to dry, trying not to peek at what they might reveal.

To print a negative, you have to load it into an

enlarger, which is the machine that shines light through the negative and exposes the image on a piece of light-sensitive paper. When you're ready to do that, you turn off the room's overhead light and turn on the safe light, open up the enlarger lens, and turn the enlarger light on, which projects the image onto the paper. From there, it's a lot of adjusting until you have the image just the way you want it. Turn off the enlarger, put in a sheet of photographic paper, turn on the enlarger for six seconds. Then it's time to slip the paper into the developer for a minute or so, and then into the stop bath for ten seconds, and then you put it into the fix. Finally you wash the paper off and hang it up to dry.

My hands shook trying to load the first negative into the enlarger. I didn't know what to expect, couldn't quite imagine what picture would emerge, but I knew it would be something amazing.

Instead, it was a picture of a hut.

"Actually," Sgt. Byrd informed me, "it's called a hootch. And it's a good picture. Your brother knows what he's doing with a camera."

Maybe. If what he was trying to do was bore

people to death. From a roll of thirty-six negatives, I counted eleven huts, nine assorted groupings of GIs—most of them sitting around with their shirts off and drinking beer—six pictures of the same dog—a white terrier with a black spot around its left eye—and eight pictures of bushes and trees. There was even a close-up of a blooming flower. A flower. I shook my head in disgust.

Now, sitting on Cindy's bed, I opened the manila envelope I'd put TJ's pictures in once they'd dried. "Here's a picture of some soldiers that are probably friends of TJ's. I think some of them are sort of cute, don't you?"

I held up the picture for Cindy to see. I was trying to act excited about it, but the fact is, the whole roll of film had been a disappointment to me. Huts and tents and soldiers waving beer cans in the general direction of the camera. Nothing worth noting, in my opinion, especially when there was a war being fought in the vicinity. If I was excited about anything, it was that I'd learned to develop and print film. I wanted to show somebody what I'd done, even if the end result wasn't all that fascinating.

"Come watch me ride my bike," Cindy said, hopping off of her bed.

"Don't you want to see the rest of TJ's photographs? He's in Vietnam, just like Mark."

Cindy crossed her arms over her chest. "I know TJ's in Vietnam. I'm not stupid. I'm not retarded like you think. I'm just special and I have a medical condition."

"I know you're not retarded," I said. "It's just we both have brothers in Vietnam, and it's this thing we have in common."

Cindy looked at me for several seconds. Then she nodded and sat back down next to me on the bed. "I like having things in common."

I showed her the rest of the pictures. The last one I pulled out of the envelope was a moon shot. "I want that one," Cindy told me, tugging the picture out of my hands. "I could put it on my wall, and then I could look at the moon any time I wanted."

"Okay." I could go back to the rec center in the morning and print another copy if I felt like it. "Are there any others you want?"

"No, just the moon."

It was one of TJ's better moons, I thought. It had a band of light around it and it sat plush in the middle, beaming, a fat full moon on a beautiful night.

"Now will you watch me ride my bike?" Cindy asked.

"Sure," I told her, tucking the pictures back into the envelope. Usually I would have found an excuse to go home, but I was feeling good. I had developed and printed a roll of film. And maybe even better than that, TJ had asked me to do it, which meant he believed I could. I don't know why he believed it, but he did. So now *we* had something in common, even though we were so far away from each other.

"Come on," Cindy groused at me from the doorway. "Let's get going!"

I picked up the envelope and followed her out the door. "Okay, okay, you don't have to be such a grouch."

But I was smiling as I said it. I guess I was in a generous mood.

seven

TJ's next so-called letter came two weeks later. I ripped open the padded envelope, hoping this time there'd be a note with some real news in it, some good old-fashioned descriptions of rifle reports or a hand grenade rolling across a jungle path, something that would give me a real feel for what it was like to be TJ right then. It might be tough for me to actually get a job as an ambulance driver in Vietnam, but if TJ would just write me a real letter, it would be like I was there in Vietnam, right beside him.

But all that envelope contained was two rolls of film in their little black canisters with their little gray caps. His letter to my parents was as boring as the one before it had been. The food was bad; the nurses were nice, a couple of them were even pretty; he'd been riding some in the medevac helicopter, which was the helicopter that went to pick up wounded soldiers. That last part had the potential to be interesting, only TJ didn't describe an actual time when he'd ridden the helicopter out to a battle scene. My seventh-grade English teacher, Mrs. Robertson, would have deducted ten points for lack of specific detail.

Because I was a natural in the darkroom, I decided to try developing the film alone, without Sgt. Byrd there to guide me through every step. I felt nervous about it, but I reasoned that I couldn't depend on Sgt. Byrd to be there to help me the entire time TJ was in Vietnam. And I didn't make a single mistake, if you don't count dropping the film spool lid in the dark closet and having to get down on my hands and knees to find it and then dropping the second roll of film in the dark, before I'd even unspooled it, and having to scramble around twenty minutes before I found it by kneeling on it.

But I didn't expose the film, and that was all that counted. When I finished getting it on the spool and into the canister and got the lid on tight, I mixed the developer and poured it into the canister. I poured out the developer after ten minutes, poured in the vinegary-smelling stop solution. After that came the fixer. Then I rinsed off all the chemicals, pulled out the negatives, and hung them up to dry from the clothesline strung across the room, and went out to talk to Private Hollister.

"I wish TJ would write me a real letter," I told him after we'd sat down across from each other at his desk and he began to deal the cards for a game of gin. "I don't even know if he got the pictures I developed for him."

"When did you send them?"

"A week ago."

"He ain't got the package yet, then. Or he's just getting it right about now."

"Well, you'd think he'd want to see how I did on the first roll of film before he sent me any more." I leaned back in my chair, thinking about how badly

I wanted to hear what TJ had to say about the job I did with his film. He'd only asked for contact sheets, where each negative was printed in miniature, so you could see all your pictures from a roll of film on one sheet of paper. I'd done a sheet for him, but I'd also done prints of each photograph.

Private Hollister picked up a card from the top of the deck. "Your pictures looked pretty good to me. Or TJ's pictures, I guess I should say. I bet he'll like them a lot. Did your folks like 'em?"

"Yeah, I guess. I mean, my mom hung two of them on the refrigerator, so I guess she liked them. This new batch looks pretty interesting, from what I can tell," I said, discarding and picking up a card from the deck. "It's hard to tell exactly what you're looking at when you're looking at a negative. Definitely people, but I think there might be some of helicopters this time."

We played five hands of gin, with Private Hollister coming out on top, three hands to two.

"I guess I'll go print those pictures now," I said. "The negatives ought to be dry. I hope there's some good stuff. Like maybe a combat picture or something. Maybe some North Vietnamese prisoners of war. Sgt. Byrd taught me some Vietnam talk when we worked on the last roll of film. Like an ambulance is called a cracker box and you call the enemy Charlie or Mr. Charles."

"You know, Jamie, there's something—" Private Hollister started, stopped, coughed. "There's just this one thing you ought—" He stopped again. "Forget it. It ain't important."

"Are you sure?" I asked him, itching to get to that film.

Private Hollister nodded. "Nothing that can't wait till later."

I made contact sheets of both rolls of film. Last time I'd printed all the pictures, but this time I decided to be more picky. Once I'd developed the contact sheets, I sat down at a table in the darkroom with a magnifying glass to go over each picture and see which ones were worth taking the time to print. As I'd thought, there were plenty of pictures of people, lots of soldiers—holding beer cans or sleeping or lying on cots reading magazines. There was a trio of pretty nurses, and the dog he'd taken a picture of before showed up again, this time with a bandanna tied around its neck.

I was starting to get bored. Since I didn't know any of the people, their pictures didn't mean anything to me. But then an image caught my eye. Three medics were carrying a wounded GI on a stretcher toward a helicopter. In the foreground was another soldier, only he was looking away from the helicopter, like he didn't want to see what was going on all around him. The wounded soldier had bandages wrapped around his chest, and there was blood seeping through them.

That was the picture I wanted to print.

It's a funny thing, printing a photograph, because when you're in the process of doing it, you're paying attention to the tiniest things, like the fingers on a hand, trying to get them to show up in sharp detail, or bringing out the shadow falling across somebody's face. Each little piece of the picture is like part of a puzzle, and the more defined you make everything, the more your picture tells a story.

For some reason, I got all involved in bringing

out the details on the soldier's face, the one who was looking away. He was probably headed back to get someone else, but the way the camera caught him, it seemed like he couldn't bear to look at the man the medics were carrying to the helicopter. Maybe because his was the only face I could really see, I kept wanting to look at it, kept wondering what he was thinking about.

And then my eyes drifted up to the wounded soldier. There was a lot of blood coming through the bandages wrapped around his chest. Did TJ know whether or not he made it to the hospital alive? Was he alive now? Back in the States? Or back in a combat zone?

I spent an hour printing the picture, trying it again and again until I felt I had it right. I brought it out to show Private Hollister. "Isn't this amazing?" I asked him, feeling excited about the work I'd done. "I mean, it's a picture of somebody who's actually been hit by the enemy. It's the real war."

"It's real, all right." Private Hollister looked awkward, like he didn't quite know what to say to me. "I mean, it's definitely a real war. Don't know if I want to look at pictures of the people who are getting killed over there, though. I've seen enough of that on TV, I guess. Heard enough about it on a day-to-day basis over the last few years."

"Did you ever know anyone who got killed there?"

Private Hollister was quiet for a minute. I wondered if he was going through a list of buddies, trying to remember if everybody was still accounted for. He cleared his throat and said, "Yeah, well, my brother Barney did. Right at the beginning, back in '65. Hardly anybody knew there was a war then, not like the way it is now, with protesters and hippies and everything."

"Your brother *died*?" For some reason, I found this answer nearly unacceptable. Private Hollister wasn't the sort of person who had a dead brother. He wasn't the least bit tragic. "Did you cry?"

He laughed and looked up in the air, like he didn't know how to answer that question and was hoping the ceiling might have some advice for him.

"I don't know why I asked that," I said quickly. "It's just if TJ died in Vietnam, I'd cry, but I'm a girl."

———

"My mom cried," Private Hollister said, sounding more comfortable all of a sudden, like the topic of girls crying was a lot easier one for him to handle. "Man, she cried a whole river. The doctor finally had to give her some pills."

"My mom has these pills the doctor gave her for bad headaches. She takes one, she sleeps for twenty-four hours straight."

"Huh," Private Hollister said, like I'd just told him something very interesting and worthwhile.

Right about then we ran out of conversation.

I put the picture down on Private Hollister's desk, picked it up again. "Well, I guess I'll go clean up in the back. I'll do some more printing tomorrow. After work, that is. Don't forget, I'm here to work."

"You're here to play cards is more like it." Private Hollister grinned.

"That, too," I agreed. Then I walked back to the darkroom to clean up the mess I'd made. I pinned the picture of the soldier back up on the line and leaned over to pick up some scraps of cut negatives off the floor. As I tossed them into the trash can, a shiver zipped down my arms to the tips of my fingers, the way it did whenever I was lying in bed in the dark and got convinced there was a ghost watching me from the corner of the room. But when I looked around the darkroom, all I saw was the picture of the soldier on the stretcher, his face peering down at me from the clothesline.

Later, when I looked at that picture again, I stared for a long time at the soldier, imagining what I would do differently if I decided to print it again. I wished I could see the soldier's face. I thought about the fact that he might have been somebody's brother. Somebody who was waiting for him to come home.

I knew that was one picture I wasn't going to show to my mother.

eight

In the weeks before TJ left to join the Army, things around our house got loud and very quiet at the same time. The loudness came from TJ yelling, "Hey, have you seen the lock to my footlocker?" from upstairs when everybody else was downstairs, or from me yelling across the hall, "Hey, TJ, I'm going to the PX, you want me to get anything on your list?" It also came from my mother, who, despite a certain talent for keeping a stiff upper lip during trying times, kept having minor emotional outbursts, like when she was doing dishes by herself in the kitchen and suddenly cried out to no one, "Whose idea was it to have this war, anyway? Whose idiotic idea was it?"

The quiet came from the Colonel.

All spring, the big mystery had been why the Colonel was so against TJ enlisting. At first I thought it was my mother who made him say all those things to TJ about how fun college would be and how it would be a shame to miss it. My mother is a former Southern belle debutante, very flowery and chock-full of good manners, but she generally gets what she wants. Only she hardly ever comes right out and forces things to happen. She's more subtle than that. It wouldn't be at all unlike her to work behind the scenes, making little suggestions to the Colonel about what he should say to TJ to get him to change his mind about enlisting.

Add that to the fact that the Colonel is 100 percent gung-ho Army, *hoo-ah,* yes sir, the last person on Earth you'd think would try to keep someone from joining up. How many times had I heard the Colonel talk about the honor of sacrifice? When we were stationed at Fort Bragg, North Carolina, he'd driven me and TJ to the veterans' hospital over in Durham one Christmas just to pay our respects to the soldiers there, a lot of whom had fought in World War II. *We owe them our gratitude and respect,* the Colonel had said. *The very least we can do is wish them a Merry Christmas.* This was a man who didn't want his son to enlist?

So it had to be my mother making the Colonel try to convince TJ to break his enlistment contract, I was sure of it. But one night, when we were sitting at the dining-room table playing Scrabble after dinner, the Colonel said, "You won't have two seconds to play tic-tac-toe where you're going, son." And my mother sighed and said, "Would you please stop, Tom? This has gone on long enough. Please honor TJ's decision."

Well, that rocked me right back in my chair. It was clear from my mother's tone of voice that the Colonel had been getting on her nerves for some time now, only up until this point she'd been too much of a lady to let it show. But if it wasn't my mother behind the Colonel's constant haranguing, what did that mean? That the Colonel himself didn't want TJ to enlist? This plain floored me. It was as if Thomas Jefferson had stood up in the middle of writing the Declaration of Independence and declared he was against democracy. It was like Thomas Alva Edison saying, "Oh, heck, what's so great about electricity after all? Let's keep using candles."

I decided to try to talk to him about it. I was at this time about nine months away from turning thirteen, and I felt I could speak to the Colonel as an equal. Also, I thought this might be an opportunity for me to make a good impression on him. Not that I thought the Colonel had a bad impression of me. He seemed to like me just fine on a day-to-day basis, and I assumed he loved me—not that anyone in my family went around saying, "I love you." But the Colonel seemed to want me to be happy, and he seemed genuinely pleased when I was happy, and that struck me as a pretty good definition of love when you got right down to it.

But it's one thing to like somebody and to love your own child. It's a whole other thing to be impressed by someone. At age twelve and a quarter, I was not actually all that impressive. I was always spilling on myself at the dinner table, and my hair never just laid down flat on my head and looked nice, and my grades were not stellar. Good in math, so-so in everything else. I did have a good arm and an ability to memorize football statistics. I was an excellent card player. But my clothes were always wrinkled and in disarray by ten in the morning. I hated extracurricular activities. There was no chance I was going to cure the common cold or rocket into outer space any time soon.

Still, I kept looking for ways to impress the Colonel. I mowed the lawn without being asked to. I babysat Cindy Lorenzo for free. I joined the junior high school pep club, even though I am not a naturally peppy person, and went to all sorts of boring junior high sports events and cheered and yelled like a person who has school spirit and a good attitude.

Why did I think it would impress the Colonel to have a man-to-man conversation about TJ, especially when I wasn't a man and what TJ did or didn't do wasn't actually my business? Well, I saw it as a taking-the-bull-by-the-horns opportunity. The Colonel was behaving in a mystifying way. I would ask him why and have an adult conversation about the pros and cons of his behavior. He would be impressed because I was acting like such a grown-up person. And, with any luck, I'd find out why he couldn't bring himself to be happy about the fact that his number one and only son had joined the Army.

Most nights after dinner, especially in spring, the Colonel liked to work in the garden until it was too dark to see. Spring was the Colonel's favorite time of year. He was a man who liked to dig in the dirt, and in the spring that's what he spent most of his free time doing. "Five-cent plant, fifty-cent hole" was his motto, which is why he had two hundred pounds of cow manure delivered fresh from the farm the minute the last frost date had passed. He'd hoe up his garden beds and work that manure in, pausing every few minutes to sniff the air and holler out, "Nothing ever smelled better!"

It was early April, and since it was Texas, the frost date had long passed and he already had plants growing, tiny ones, so he was spending his evenings patrolling for miniscule pests and the first bud of a weed that dared to show its face in his garden beds. He'd cuss them and then dispose of them. I was surprised he never hung up little dead slugs around the perimeters, just to show their friends what happened to trespassers.

"I heard if you put out bowls of beer, it'll draw the slugs away from your plants," I told him as I walked out into the backyard from the kitchen. "They like the beer so much, they crawl into the bowl and drown."

"You read that in *Time* magazine, Sport?" The Colonel looked up from where he was spraying pesticide on his baby tomato plants.

"Probably. I'd sure like to see a drunk slug, wouldn't you?"

"Only if it were a dead one." The Colonel stood up and walked to get the hose. "Why don't you go on weed patrol? I can't believe how fast those suckers come up in Texas. Back east, you don't see your first serious weeds until May."

I went over to the bed next to the one he was watering. "I was wondering something, sir,"

I started out, not sure exactly what I meant to ask him. "About TJ enlisting?"

"You're not thinking about enlisting too, are you?"

"I would if they'd let me, sir."

He looked at me and grinned. "I don't doubt it."

"I guess what I'm curious about is why you don't want TJ to enlist. I mean, you love the Army more than anybody I know."

The Colonel wiped his forehead with the back of his hand. "If TJ wants to join the Army when he's done with college, I'd be all for that. He might think about joining ROTC when he's in college. The Army can help him pay for medical school. But he needs to go to college first, before he joins. He needs to grow up some more. TJ's not ready for the Army."

TJ needed to grow up? That was like saying the Eiffel Tower needed to get a little taller. TJ was more grown up than most adults I knew. And who had spent more time planning battles and executing strategies than TJ? Nobody except maybe Douglas A. MacArthur or General George Patton.

"Are you scared something might happen to

him?" This was the one explanation I'd been able to come up with on my own. Sure, the Colonel was a big, tough guy, but even big, tough guys don't want their sons to get killed.

"There's a weed to your left, looks like pokeweed." The Colonel leaned across me and plucked it out. "You let pokeweed get too big, you'll never get it under control."

End of conversation. Obviously, the Colonel wasn't telling the whole story about why he didn't want TJ to enlist. The only thing I knew for sure after that conversation was that he wasn't planning on telling it any time soon.

He still tried to try to talk TJ out of enlisting, though, using every one of his formidable talents of persuasion during the thirty-day window when TJ could have still ripped up his enlistment contract. He'd joked, cajoled, argued, offered bribes both material and monetary. He somehow got his hands on a recent University of Georgia yearbook and took to perusing it during dinner, making comments about all the interesting activities one might get involved in at college, and how to his eyes it appeared that all the pretty girls headed to Athens, Georgia, in the fall for college. "You've heard of Georgia peaches, haven't you, son?" he'd ask. "I got me one"—and here he winked at my mother—"and you could get yourself one too."

TJ, for his part, listened, laughed, nodded, argued, and rolled his eyes, but he did not budge and he did not change his mind. Then, one day, just like that, the window closed, and TJ was in the Army, no turning back. In two months, at the end of May, he'd report to an MEPS, a Military Entrance Processing Station, in San Antonio, where he would present all the necessary paperwork and take his physical, then choose his MOS, his Military Occupational Specialty, which he had already decided would be in the Medical Service Corps. He'd go through basic training, come home for a few days, and then, more than likely, get shipped off to Vietnam sometime in July.

So there wasn't much left for the Colonel to say. During those couple of months before TJ had to report, life mostly went on as normal, TJ getting ready to graduate from high school, me dreading the end of seventh grade, when I'd have to say good-bye to my best friends and begin searching around for new ones. The only thing different was that the Colonel wasn't talking. Oh, he'd say the normal things, like, "Please pass the butter" or "Did you finish your homework?" but usually having the Colonel in the house was like having an opera going on. He was big, he was loud, he had a lot to talk about. So when he started getting quiet and stopped saying anything, well, it felt like we were living in a library. Or a morgue.

One Sunday afternoon I was lying across my bed, alternately imagining I was an ambulance driver in a combat zone and that I was a character in an Archie comic, a new girl who wasn't an idiot like Veronica but was still good-looking, when TJ's voice boomed across the hall. "Hey, Jamie, want to look at some pictures?"

I slowly rolled off the bed and shuffled over to TJ's room. It was a wreck. He'd been trying to get organized, since there would only be two days between graduation the next week and when he left for San Antonio to get processed into the Army. So there were boxes everywhere and a footlocker spilling over with the things he had to take to basic training: underwear, thong shower shoes, socks, a shoe shine kit. And then there were stacks of photographs, which he'd gotten the brilliant idea of sorting through and filing in folders before he left. It was the sort of plan that seems good when you come up with it, but after about twenty minutes you're sorry you started.

Still, TJ looked happy sitting on a chair in the middle of his room, surrounded by piles of pictures. "Look at this one of Mom," he said, holding up a picture of my mother looking up from the book she was reading, *Pride and Prejudice*, her favorite novel of all time, her forehead furrowed with deep lines, as though they had drawn them on. Her expression was clearly saying, *I get five minutes to myself all day, so you best back out of the room slowly and leave me be.*

"That's not going to be her favorite picture in the world," I said. "I'd think twice before showing it to her."

"Yeah, maybe you're right." TJ put the photograph down on the floor and picked up another, this one of the Colonel getting out of the car after work. It was what they call a candid shot, which means the Colonel didn't know TJ was taking it. His face was halfway in the shadows of the carport, but the sunlight caught the shine of his polished boots. I was surprised by how tired he looked.

"When did you take that one?"

TJ shrugged. "A couple of weeks ago, I guess. He looks like an old man, huh? I guess that's another one not quite right for the family album."

I took the picture from TJ and examined it more closely. There were bags under the Colonel's eyes. He was carrying a briefcase, but by the slump of his shoulders, you'd think he was carrying a suitcase full of cement.

There was no doubt about it. The Colonel looked like a man who hated his job.

nine

Working at the rec center, I was learning more about Vietnam all the time. It was in the air you breathed if you were spending your days around GIs, some of whom had already done their tour, some who were gearing up to go, and a whole bunch who had their fingers crossed the war would be over before their units got called up.

Sgt. Byrd gave me daily vocabulary lessons. Sometimes it was like he was still in-country, and there were days I thought maybe he wanted to go back. Every once in a while he made me feel scared, the way his face got dark and cloudy over something he saw in one of TJ's pictures. But there wasn't ever a time when he didn't want to talk. He was a big talker, someone who liked words for words' sake, the sound of them, the way you can pile them up in your mouth and make a poem if you spill them out the right way.

"If you recall, you call that a cracker box," he said, pointing to a picture of an ambulance I'd printed from TJ's fourth roll of film. "The *bac-si* rides in the cracker box—'*bac-si*' is what you call a medic, it's a Vietnamese word—or they go in the traveling medicine show, which is what you call the medevac helicopter."

"How come they do that?" I asked. "I mean, how come they make up words for everything that already has its own word?"

"I don't know. Maybe it makes it less real, more like a cartoon, something that's not happening directly to you. Or else it's just fun to do it. The human animal is an endless creative creature, in my experience."

So I learned "chop chop" was food and a "daily-daily" was the antimalaria pill GIs had to take. Medics were called "Docs" and "band-aids" and "*bac-si*," and infantrymen were called "grunts." An Army helmet was a "steel pot," and camouflage uniforms were nicknamed "tiger suits." If you were KIA you'd been killed in action, and if you were KBA, you'd been killed by artillery. A "glad bag" was a body bag. "Expectants" were wounded soldiers who were expected to die.

"What did they call you?" I asked Sgt. Byrd when the vocabulary lesson got too filled with body bags and wounded soldiers for my comfort.

He grinned. "I was a 1st Cav grunt and a Cheap Charlie because I never spent any money in the bars. Other than that, mostly I got called Ted and a few other names too improper to repeat. Oh, and Kodak. I got called Kodak." He held up his camera bag. "For the obvious reasons."

Sgt. Byrd was not my only source on the lifestyle and culture of the Vietnam War, however. There were also my students.

Just like Private Hollister had said, there were soldiers who wanted to learn how to develop and print their own pictures, and now I was the resident expert, if you didn't count Sgt. Byrd, and since he didn't actually work at the rec center, I didn't count him.

The first soldier I helped was Corporal Yarrow. Cpl. Yarrow was the saddest-looking human being I'd ever seen, hangdog eyes worse than a basset hound's, bushy black eyebrows that sagged to a point above the bridge of his nose. That he always had a joke or a smart-aleck comment coming out of the side of his mouth was my first surprise about him. That he was so smart he could cuss in German, French, and Spanish without anybody having ever taught him how was my second.

His first surprise about me was that I was twelve years old. He'd come hollering into the darkroom, "Hollister said somebody back here could help me with this film? That wouldn't be you, would it?"

"It's me, all right." I was hanging some prints on the line to dry. "What do you need help with?"

He came over and stood beside me. "Nice pictures. Who took 'em?"

"My brother. He's with the 51st Medical Company, in Phu Bai."

"Oh, yeah? I was with 1st Battalion, 69th Armor, in the Binh Dinh province. I was a gunner."

"A gunner?"

"Yeah, a tank gunner."

I took that in. Tanks are serious business. Shooting a gun rapid-fire from the top of a tank is very serious business. It looks cool in the movies, but in real life it has to be a tough job. But Cpl. Yarrow didn't look tough. He just looked like a sad, nice guy.

"So anyway," Cpl. Yarrow continued, "I went fishing down at Big Bend while I was on leave a couple of weekends ago, and the only thing I caught was what I caught on film. If you catch my drift."

"Fish weren't biting?"

"They might have been biting something, but it wasn't anything dangling off the end of my hook. Still, the scenery was great and the beer was flowing, and I have lots of warm and fuzzy memories." He held up his film canister. "Not too fuzzy, I hope. I was gonna drop the film off at the PX, but then this friend convinced me I ought to develop it myself, since it's black-and-white film, and he thinks I need a hobby."

So I taught Cpl. Yarrow what to do, and his pictures came out great, so then he brought in his buddy, Pvt. Garza, the one who told him to develop his own film in the first place, and Cpl. Yarrow and I taught Pvt. Garza.

I was a good teacher, which surprised me. I am not the world's most patient person, and I don't always do a great job of translating the thoughts in my head into words. But it was easy talking about how to develop film and print pictures. It helped that Cpl. Yarrow and Pvt. Garza picked up on everything fast and found the process interesting. I remembered what Sgt. Byrd told me the first day we worked in the darkroom together, that he was a process guy. I knew what he meant now. Every part of the developing process was interesting to me. Whenever I made a discovery—that a certain kind of paper worked better, or that I got better results if the developing chemicals were a degree or two cooler—I was in a good mood for the rest of the day.

On the days I printed TJ's pictures, I always

drew an audience. It was like Private Hollister had put a sign out front: VIETNAM PICTURES ON VIEW TODAY IN DARKROOM. He always knew when I came in with a roll of TJ's film, and he'd always be the first one back to take a look. "Don't show me nothing bloody," he'd say when I told him the pictures were up on the line. "I can turn on the TV if I feel the need to see blood."

Private Hollister especially liked TJ's pictures of the moon and of pretty nurses. "You think he's got a girlfriend over there yet?" he asked one day, studying a blond WAC holding a cat.

"How would I know? He just sends me film. He doesn't write me letters."

Private Hollister studied the photographs. "I'd say he's writing you a letter with every picture he takes. Does he write letters to your folks?"

I nodded. "They're boring, though. Mostly they're about the food and the bugs."

"See? He's sending you the real stuff. I bet you don't show all these pictures to your parents, do you? I bet you hide some of 'em away."

"What makes you say that?"

"'Cause you know TJ don't want your folks to see 'em. If he wanted them to see all this stuff, he'd send the film to your mom, get her to get it processed at the PX. Don't cost but a few dollars."

Private Hollister was right. I'd only shown certain ones of TJ's pictures to my parents, pictures of dogs and mess halls and big jungle plants. But I'd known without him having to tell me that TJ wouldn't want me to show them everything. With each roll of film TJ sent me, there were fewer blond WAC's and more soldiers missing arms and legs. More medevac helicopters. More dust and dirt and chaos.

One day after I'd developed a roll of film and had the negatives hanging from the line to dry, I realized I was squinting as I examined them. It was as though I only half wanted to see what was there.

It was as though I was scared to look any closer.

I thought about waiting until the next day to print the pictures, even though it was early and Private Hollister said there wasn't much for me to do that day. I had all the time in the world to print pictures, but I found myself cleaning up, wiping down tables, measuring out more fixer, inventorying chemicals.

Finally I made myself slip the first negative into the enlarger. What emerged on the paper was a picture of a GI in a wheelchair, his right leg amputated at the knee and wrapped in a white bandage. He looked so much like TJ, I gasped and took a step backward. I had to force myself to look again and see for sure that it wasn't my brother in the wheelchair, that it was someone I'd never seen before in my life.

I decided to print the rest of the pictures later.

Some of the soldiers who looked at TJ's pictures had been in Vietnam, and the pictures reminded them of all sorts of things. "You ever heard of rice paddy stew?" one guy asked me, looking at a photograph of guys eating at the mess hall. "You take your C rations, like the beef and the franks and beans, throw in some cheese spread and crackers and rice, add a bunch of Tabasco sauce, and mix it all up and cook it. Nine times out of ten it's better than whatever they're serving in the mess."

The soldiers who had never been to Vietnam were the ones who got quiet when they saw TJ's pictures. Pvt. Garza was like that. He was on the quiet side anyway, which made him a good side-kick for Cpl. Yarrow, but he got downright silent when he looked at TJ's photographs.

"The war's almost over," Cpl. Yarrow told him one day when he was standing in front of a picture of a medevac helicopter lifting off, the sun setting behind it, dust billowing out in huge clouds beneath the propellers. "Chances are you'll never get sent. Don't worry about it, man."

Pvt. Garza shook his head. "It's not over yet."

"Any day, that's what they're saying." Cpl. Yarrow put his hand on Pvt. Garza's shoulder. "Any day."

There were afternoons I'd feel shaky leaving the rec center, anxious and a little bit nervous, and I just needed to get it out of my system, so I'd go to Cindy's house and tell her what I was learning about Vietnam. She was halfway interested in some of the things, not at all interested in others. Mostly she wanted to know if TJ had sent me more pictures of the moon. There was one in every roll, and I'd always make Cindy a print. By early August she had a collection of them taped to her wall.

"Does Mark write you letters?" I asked one afternoon, sitting on Cindy's bed, Brutus nestled in my lap. "Does he tell you anything about what it's like to be over there?"

"He writes a big letter that's for everyone in my family," Cindy told me. "He tells us about different things he sees, like the animals and the different kind of flowers."

"Do you, you know, ever worry about him?" I hugged Brutus close to me.

"Why would I worry about Mark? He's an Army soldier. Fighting in wars is his job."

I nodded. Fighting was a soldier's job. Everybody knew that.

It was just, somewhere down there in the pit of my stomach, I was starting to think that I didn't like fighting as much as I thought I did. I was starting to feel like I wished I hadn't told TJ to go.

ten

By mid-August Private Hollister and I were neck and neck in our race to see who would be the gin rummy champ of Fort Hood, Texas. And we weren't the only ones paying attention to the competition. All the rec center regulars checked in at least once a week to see who was in the lead. They'd pull Private Hollister's notebook right out of his top desk drawer and run their fingers down the rows of numbers, adding it all up. Most of them were rooting for me, because I was so much younger and a girl, I guess.

The closer it got to Labor Day, the more often we'd draw a crowd when we sat down to play. Even

Sgt. Byrd would come out of the darkroom from time to time to watch. "Play 'em as they lay, my young friend, hit him where it hurts, don't let the crumbheads get you down," he'd say, or something else so Sgt. Byrd–like I'd know it was him with my eyes closed.

"So when's your last day, anyway?" Private Hollister asked me one morning while we were trying to get some actual work done. I was underneath a pool table picking up beer can tabs and cigarette butts. Apparently there'd been quite a crowd the night before, soldiers from the 1st Armored Division, whose units were being sent to Vietnam.

"Friday before Labor Day, I guess," I called up to him from the floor. I picked up another cigarette butt and popped it into a paper bag. "I wonder if any of those guys ever heard of that useful invention known as an ashtray," I said, crawling out from under the pool table and rattling the bag at Private Hollister. "It comes in handy, I've heard."

"Ah, you know how it is when a guy's being sent off to war." Private Hollister leaned against the mop he was using to clean up spilled beer off the floor. "He gets a little wild. Mostly they're just scared, I guess, and covering it up by drinking and yelling."

"I guess. Still, now my hands stink and I think I'm about to come down with asthma."

"You don't come down with asthma. Asthma's just something you've got. It's a condition. I had it when I was a kid."

I stood up and walked over to the trash can. "Why do you want to know when my last day of work is, anyway?"

Private Hollister grinned. "I'm working up a strategy, and I need to know how many days I got to beat you fair and square. Your last day of work's gonna be our official last day of playing gin, the way I see things."

"If I win, it is. But if I lose, I'll be coming by after school."

"Doubt I'll be here much longer after Labor Day. I'll go back to my unit around then."

"What do you mean, your unit?"

Private Hollister began pushing his mop along the length of the floor. "Rec center's a temporary assignment for me. I'm a radio operator, 1st Signal Troop, but they needed somebody here this summer and I was the one who got pulled for the duty. They got another guy coming from Fort Sill sometime in September; he'll take over here and I'll go back to where I came from."

Then he stopped mopping and looked over at me. "You think your dad knows who I am? I mean, have you ever mentioned me to him?"

"Yeah, of course. I've been keeping him updated on our games and everything."

"What kind of stuff do you tell him? I mean, good things? Things that would make him think I was a good guy or a good worker or whatever?"

I laughed. "What are you talking about? Why do you care what the Colonel thinks about you?"

Private Hollister put the mop away in the supply closet and walked over to his desk before answering me. He picked up our game notebook and held it like it was a good-luck charm. "There's some rumors going around post. About how they're going to send some guys from 1st Signal Troop over to Vietnam pretty soon. Radio operators."

My mouth went dry. "That's you."

Private Hollister slapped the notebook against his knee. "Yep, that's me. It's just a rumor that's been going around, but I wondered if your dad had said anything about it to you. Because he has some control over that situation."

"The Colonel has some control over who goes to Vietnam?"

"Well, yeah, from Hood, I mean. If they're gonna move some troops, then Col. Dexter is part of the group that says who's going. He's the chief of staff, right? The adjutant general reports to him, gives him the list of who he thinks should go, Col. Dexter signs the orders. Your daddy's a big-shot wheeler-dealer, I don't need to tell you that."

Private Hollister put down the notebook. Then he walked to the pool table and picked up a stick, examining it as if it were an item of some interest to him. "If they send me to Vietnam, my mom's gonna go nuts."

"They won't send you," I insisted. They couldn't send him. His brother had already died there. It wouldn't be fair to send Private Hollister, too.

Private Hollister looked up at me. "They will if they want to."

"But I don't want them to."

That made Private Hollister laugh. "I figured you'd think this was the opportunity of a lifetime for me. An all-expenses-paid trip to Vietnam. Maybe round trip, maybe not. Go live the life of a real soldier."

I looked down at my feet. "I guess."

"Well, do me a favor, okay? Let me know if you hear anything. Your dad might say something to you, since he knows we work together."

"That wouldn't be Army protocol. The Colonel doesn't tell me anything about work. Nothing like that, anyway."

Private Hollister lined up a shot on the pool table. "Maybe you could ask him, then. I mean, ask him what he knows."

I looked at the clock. It was almost one. I needed to be at the Lorenzos' house in fifteen minutes, to babysit Cindy while Mrs. Lorenzo went to the commissary. "I have to go now," I said. "I have a babysitting job this afternoon."

"Think about it, Jamie. If it's gonna happen, I need to know. I got to get prepared, you know, in my mind."

As I walked out the doors, the sudden crack of the balls scattering across the pool table made me flinch. I remembered something that Sgt. Byrd had told me, that he dreamed about Vietnam almost every night, and some nights he woke up to find himself crouched in the dark between the bunks in his barracks, his whole body alert, listening.

Listening for what? I'd asked him.

The sound before the sound, he'd told me. *The sound that comes right before the sound of everything getting blown to smithereens.*

I did not want Private Hollister to go to Vietnam.

I didn't want anyone else I knew going to Vietnam. But Private Hollister was the one who I might be able to help.

In my hand I held one very important card.

I made a fist.

I got ready to knock.

eleven

When I got to Cindy's, she wanted to put on a ballet
for me, and I said sure. But I barely paid attention,
I was so busy thinking about what I would say to the
Colonel. Somehow I had to convince him to keep
Private Hollister at Fort Hood. But how do you ask
the most full-out Army man in the Army for a favor
like that?

My biggest obstacle was plain and simple
Army protocol, which of course the Colonel was a
stickler for. You did things a certain way, played
by the Army rules at all times, followed the chain
of command. If the rumors were true, some bigwig over in Vietnam had decided he needed more

radio operators, and some other bigwig, probably at the Pentagon, looked through his files and came up with the great idea of sending a few from 1st Signal Troop, Fort Hood. The paperwork would be drawn up by a clerk, copied in triplicate, rubber-stamped, and sent over to Fort Hood and up the chain until it reached the Colonel, who would sign it, unless there was an excellent reason not to. He did not mess with protocol. Period.

"You aren't watching me!" Cindy stood in front of me, hands planted on her hips. "You're looking at me, but you're not watching! I know, because that's what my dad does too."

"I was watching, really," I lied. "You looked really good. I like how you twirl around."

Cindy nodded, like she agreed that she was quite a fine twirler. "My mom says if I keep practicing I can get real ballerina shoes with hard toes. And maybe I can take lessons over at Miss Marie's Dance Studio in Killeen."

"You want to show me some more?"

Cindy sat down next to me on the couch. "No, I'm tired now. And I'm very sad."

"Why are you sad?"

"Because my mom told me Mark won't be home for Christmas. He'll still be fighting in the war."

"TJ won't be home for Christmas either," I said, realizing it for the first time. What would it be like, to go downstairs Christmas morning by myself, to see if Santa Claus (aka the Colonel) had come? What would it be like without TJ behind me, excited as a little kid, even when all Santa had left him the last few years were clothes and new sports equipment?

"Do you think Santa Claus goes to Vietnam?" Cindy asked.

I nodded. "Sure. He goes everywhere. When we lived in Germany, he came to Germany. He'll go to Vietnam, too."

Cindy sat up. "I was born in Germany. I was born in West Berlin, West Germany, in a United States Army hospital. I was born in Berlin, Germany, but I'm still an American, so don't tell me I'm not." She elbowed me in the ribs to emphasize her point.

"I was born in Heidelberg," I told her, moving over a few feet so she couldn't get me again. "But

I'm an American too. All Army kids born in Germany are."

"A boy at school called me a Nazi. He said I was like Hitler." Cindy chewed on a cuticle, her eyes darting around the room. "I told him he was crazy. I said, 'You're so crazy it makes me hate you.'"

"That's happened to me," I said. "Kids calling me a Nazi. They think it's funny."

Cindy and I looked at each other. Now we had two things in common: brothers in Vietnam and being called Nazis by jerks.

It was quite a list.

"We're Americans, you and me," Cindy said, and clapped her right hand over her heart. "We're not stupid Nazis."

"Not us," I agreed.

We sat there quietly for a minute, with a friendly feeling around us. I started wondering how complicated Cindy's thoughts got about things. She knew Mark was fighting in Vietnam, but did she know what war looked like? Was she scared he wouldn't come home, or that he'd come home missing an arm or a leg?

Why, I suddenly wondered, was TJ sending me pictures of soldiers missing arms and legs?

Why was TJ sending me pictures?

Was he trying to scare me? Or was he just trying to tell me that war wasn't anything like the way we'd dreamed it, playing with our little green Army men under the trees?

I looked down at my hands, and suddenly I got it. Of course that's what TJ was trying to tell me. He was smart enough to know I wouldn't believe it if all he sent me were words. He'd had to show me with pictures.

Cindy jumped up. "I have a present for you! Stay right here!"

I imagined Cindy traipsing back into the room with some papier-mâché glob she'd made at the art camp her mom had taken her to the week before. But when she returned, she was carrying Brutus.

"You can take him," Cindy said. "Because I was thinking about it, and I remember that I have something else from you to keep. I have all the moon pictures you gave me. I don't need so many things from you, only one or two at a time."

"Things of mine?"

"Yes. And then I pretend we're sisters who share things."

I took this opportunity to study my toes and feel guilty for all the times I could have been nicer to Cindy. I felt like I should do something right then, like give Cindy a little hug or tell her I thought of us as sisters too. But I didn't have it in me, which I understood then and still understand to this day to be a sorry thing.

Then Cindy smiled at me. "Did you know I used to be a princess?"

"You're not a princess anymore?"

She shook her head. "No, I've decided I'd rather be president of the United States. You can do more things when you're president. Did you know I can be president, even though I was born in Germany? It's a law that says it. Nobody can tell me I can't."

"They'd be stupid to try," I agreed.

She sat down and leaned toward me so that her face was close to mine. She looked left, then right, then whispered, "I'm going to be president so I can make them send Mark home. My mom keeps crying. She says she's going to kill herself if he dies in that war."

"She said that to you?"

Cindy put her finger to her lips. "Shhh. No, she said it to Daddy when they thought I was asleep, only I was spying. She didn't even say it. She screamed it. I was very frightened. But if I was president I wouldn't be frightened, because I could bring Mark home. And TJ, too, if you want me to."

"Sure," I said. "That would be good."

But the funny thing was, it almost made me feel sad to say it. Because I knew that if I wanted TJ home, then I had lost my good feelings about the war forever. I had lost the excitement that used to get me so wound up I could hardly calm back down again for hours. I lost the green Army men under the shady trees and the thrill I felt when I imagined being an ambulance driver in a combat zone. I lost *hooah* and *combat ready, sir*.

And, when you got right down to it, if I lost all those things, I had practically lost my own self.

Which is a sad and depressing thought to have.

And I would have kept having it, except Cindy

handed me Brutus, the first real present TJ had ever given me.

Making me learn my way around the darkroom had been the second.

So maybe I wasn't so lost after all.

twelve

When TJ had come home for a few days after basic training, he'd looked like a completely different person.

He looked like a soldier.

I was almost scared to talk to him. Because I could tell he was a changed person, and I knew that whatever he'd gone through in basic training had made him stronger and harder, more ready for war. It made me feel like a little kid just to stand beside him. I figured that's what I was compared to him, a kid, and I figured that when he got back from Vietnam it would be like there were twenty years between us instead of just five, and we might not have anything to say, we'd be so different from each other.

When he got back, he would have been in a real war.

Probably the closest TJ and I had ever been was when he was twelve and I was seven. I was old enough and smart enough by then to do stuff with him, and he was still enough of a kid that he could include a seven-year-old in his plans. Those were our best war days, when we kept notebooks of make-believe battles and ran home from General MacArthur Elementary School, where TJ was in sixth grade and I was in second, so we could set up our Army guys and test out our strategies against the enemy, which was commanded by Bobby Kerner and his little brother Charles.

In a way, it's like we'd been soldiers together. I wondered if he still remembered how that felt. One thing I knew for sure when I saw him after basic training was that he'd forget the old days soon enough, if he hadn't already. He was headed for a real combat zone.

"I've been assigned to the 51st Medical Company, based in Phu Bai," he reported at the dinner table. "We ship out next Tuesday."

My mother paled. "That soon?"

"From what they're telling us, they need all the help they can get over there, as fast as they can get it."

Then TJ leaned back in his chair and looked at the Colonel. "Sir," he said, "I need you to do something for me."

All this time the Colonel had been listening, but not saying anything. Now he folded his arms across his chest and said, "What do you need me to do, son?"

"I need you to act like you're proud of me."

The Colonel looked like TJ had punched him in the gut. It was the most outright look of surprise I'd ever seen on his face. It took him a minute to gather himself enough to say, "Of course I'm proud of you, TJ."

"You just think I'm making a mistake."

"We're past all that, son," the Colonel said, sounding surer of himself now. "I'm with you a hundred percent. I'm just trying to get used to the idea of you being a soldier. I'll tell you what, you sure look like one. You remind me of myself in my prime. Son, you're going to have to beat the women off you with a stick."

The Colonel shook his head. "Asking me if I'm proud of you. How could I not be proud of you?"

TJ looked down at the table, but I could tell he was smiling, like that's all he needed the Colonel to say.

After that, everything broke loose, especially the Colonel's tongue. The man could talk some talk, and that night we got an earful. Someone had turned the opera back on.

"Now, you want to talk about a man who looked good in his first uniform," the Colonel said, leaning back until his chair tipped. He turned to my mother. "Tell these children, Jeannie-poo, what a handsome rascal I was when you first met me." When my mother just shook her head and laughed, he turned back to me and TJ. "Oh, she's too embarrassed. You never saw a woman throw herself at a man the way your mother threw herself at me."

"Oh, Tom," my mother said, blushing, even

though this was approximately the eight thousandth time the Colonel had told us the story about the dance where he and my mother met. "I don't think that's exactly what happened."

The Colonel winked. "Don't buy this little modest act of hers. She was brazen that night. Shameless might be the better word for it."

I slipped into the Colonel's story like it was a comfortable pair of old sneakers. I could have told the whole thing word for word, acted it out with all the Colonel's winks and asides, I knew it so well. I glanced at TJ, who was grinning like a kid, suddenly not looking so combat ready. I knew he was thinking the same thing I was: It was good to have the old Colonel back.

We went out in the backyard after dinner to toss around the football—even my mother, who not only had an amazing wealth of knowledge about the Washington Redskins, the Colonel's A-one, number one football team, but was also a fairly accomplished wide receiver.

"All right, everybody go out for a long pass," the Colonel commanded, and the rest of us ran toward an imaginary end zone, across the heat-blasted grass, past the tomatoes and the black-eyed Susans. The Colonel lobbed one at my mother, but it flew over her head and went bouncing off into the grass. TJ scooped up the ball and spiraled it back to the Colonel, who shot it to me.

I pulled that baby out of the air and made a beeline for the line of floribunda roses the Colonel had planted at the edge of our yard. They were big, showy flowers, the babies of the garden, threatening to fall down and die if you didn't bow to their every whim. I squinted my eyes and pretended they were the opposing team's defensive line, veered left, feinted right, and dove through a gap in the middle.

"That's my girl!" the Colonel yelled from the other end of the yard. "You show me Jamie Dexter, and I'll show you a girl who can play some football!"

I rolled onto my back and smiled up at the sky. At that very minute everything was right with my world.

But TJ was only home for the weekend. On Monday we drove him to the airport to put him on the plane for California. In California he'd board an Army transport for Vietnam. It was finally happening. I walked next to TJ through the airport, proud to be seen with him in his combat fatigues and polished-up boots, an olive-green duffel bag slung over his shoulder.

My mother, of course, started to cry when we reached TJ's gate, but she tried to act like she wasn't. She stood up straight and pretended to brush something off of TJ's shoulder. "You be sure to eat, TJ," she said before a half sob got caught in her throat. "I don't want you getting too thin."

TJ kissed her on the cheek. "I will, Mom. I'll eat everything they put in front of me, I promise."

The Colonel shook TJ's hand. "No heroics, son. Just do your job. Make us proud."

"Yes, sir."

I didn't know what to do. We weren't a family of huggers, but I felt stupid just standing there. Finally I stuck out my hand, and TJ took it. We shook solemnly.

"Write me letters," I told him. "I want to know everything that happens to you."

TJ leaned over and ruffled my hair. "I'll keep in touch," he promised.

He started for the gate. I ran after him. "Hey, TJ," I yelled. "Pathfinders!"

TJ turned around and saluted. "Combat ready!"

And then he walked through the gateway and disappeared.

Once TJ was out of sight, the Colonel sighed and shook his head. "The only way out is through," he said to nobody in particular.

"The only way out of what, Tom?" my mother asked him.

"The whole damn thing." The Colonel began walking toward the car. My mother and I trailed behind him. I for one didn't know what he was talking about, and I didn't much care. I was wound up tighter than a German clock. TJ was going to Vietnam. My brother was going to war.

Just like we'd always dreamed of.

thirteen

The Colonel was in the backyard when I got home from Cindy's. He liked to sit out there before dinner, to admire all of his botanical accomplishments. Usually he didn't do more than gaze reverently at his flowers, since my mother hated anyone to come to the dinner table dirty, but today he was underneath a forest of tea roses, pruning.

I sat down on the grass beside him and plucked a few blades. I didn't know how to say what I wanted to say. I needed a strategy, but I didn't have one. I knew I was about to ask something impossible. How do you go about doing that?

"Hand me my pruning shears, would you?" the

Colonel called from where he was kneeling deep beneath the leaves. "She's getting out of control down here."

I passed the Colonel his shears, handle first, the way he'd taught me years before, when I'd wanted to be his garden assistant, just like TJ. It had been a boring job that consisted mostly of fetching the Colonel glasses of ice water and every once in a while mixing up a brew of fish emulsion and manure tea. I'd quit after a few Saturdays. That tea stunk to high heaven.

Sitting back, I took a deep breath and plunged in. "You think the war's going to be over soon, sir?"

The Colonel pulled his long frame out from underneath the roses. "It's gone on as long as it needs to," he said, sitting up and wiping some crumbs of dirt off his cheek. "But it'll take some time to get out of there."

Okay. Next question. "Do you think it's right for the Army to send someone to war whose brother has already been killed in the war?"

"Was this person drafted, or did he enlist?"

"Enlisted." I hoped this was the better answer.

"An enlisted man has chosen the military, and he's responsible for fulfilling the duties of his enlistment agreement. It might be taken into consideration that his brother has been killed, but that doesn't mean he won't be sent if he's needed."

The Colonel stood. Pieces of mulch clung to his pants legs, old combat fatigues he wore around the house on weekends. He leaned down to brush them off. "You hear of men enlisting after their brothers have been killed in war, because they want to have a crack at the enemy. Revenge. I don't know if that's a good reason to enlist or not, but it makes for some pretty motivated soldiers."

"I don't think Private Hollister's after revenge."

The Colonel gave me a look. "Hollister? Your rec center buddy? Is that who we're talking about?"

"Private Hollister heard that they were sending radio operators from 1st Signal Troop to Vietnam." I stood up and immediately wished I were taller. The Colonel might take me more seriously if I weren't such a runt compared to him. "But he thinks it's going to be really hard on his mother if he goes, since his brother died there. And he says you're the one who signs the orders. I figured if you didn't sign his orders, he wouldn't have to go."

It wasn't the A-number-one argument I'd been hoping to make, but it laid the cards on the table. "I'm asking you not to sign his orders, sir," I finished up. "I know it goes against Army protocol, but it would mean a lot to me if you didn't sign them."

"You're asking me not to sign his orders?" The Colonel's voice was flat, disbelieving.

I nodded.

The Colonel scratched his head, then brushed back his hair with his hand. "Who do you think I am? Tell me that, Sport. Who do you think I am? Do you think I'm Santa Claus?"

"You used to be, remember?" I was scrambling, trying hard as I could to win the Colonel to my side. "Mom told us that you used to get up on the roof and jingle bells and stomp around like a reindeer."

The Colonel didn't say anything. He sat down in a lawn chair in the middle of the yard. He rubbed his eyes, put his hands down in his lap, then stretched his legs out and shoved his hands in his pockets.

He looked vaguely confused, like he wasn't sure what he was doing in this particular backyard on this particular Friday afternoon in this particular century.

"Back when TJ enlisted, when it was all a done deal, I made a call to an old buddy of mine," the Colonel said, sounding like he was about a hundred years old and a hundred miles away. "Just got his first star. Used to be Col. Sudner, now he's General Sudner. Next time I see him, I'll have to salute the guy. He's at Fort Jackson, Adjutant General's Corps, Personnel Command. I asked him to make sure TJ didn't get shipped over to Vietnam, to pull whatever strings he could. Man, he chewed me out, up one side and down the other. 'Dexter, you damn so-and-so,' he says. 'You want your son kept out of Vietnam so somebody else's son can go and get himself killed?'"

"The Sudners were at Fort Leavenworth," I said. I couldn't focus on what the Colonel was telling me. I couldn't quite take in the fact that the Colonel had tried to pull strings to keep TJ out of Vietnam. That went against protocol. It went against everything he'd ever told me about the Army way of doing things. Honor, duty, sacrifice, wasn't that what he'd been preaching to me all my life? But all I said was, "I remember Col. Sudner. He has a scar on his cheek, from where a dog bit him."

The Colonel didn't seem to hear me. "Maybe I ought to be ashamed. Sudner sure thinks so. But it's a worthless war, and I don't want any son of mine anywhere near it." He looked up at me. "I'd let somebody else die for TJ, God forgive me, but I would."

"It's a worthless war?" My mouth hung open. The Colonel was calling Vietnam a worthless war?

"We got into it for the right reasons," the Colonel said, leaning forward and looking straight at me, like he needed me to believe him. "That's what all those antiwar types don't understand. They don't understand that the Soviets and the communist Chinese are a real threat to our security. We can't let 'em have Southeast Asia."

The Colonel sat back in his chair and frowned. "Problem is, we don't know what we're doing over there. We're in over our heads. It's a jungle war against an enemy that's just plain smarter than we are when it comes to that kind of fighting. If we had any sense, we'd admit defeat and get out. Save a lot of lives that way."

I sat down on the grass. The tips of my fingers and toes felt numb. "Did you tell TJ that?"

"I told him over and over. He wouldn't listen. He's eighteen and thinks he knows everything there is to know."

"Does he know you tried to keep him out of Vietnam?"

"You're the only one in this family who knows that. Your mother doesn't even know." The Colonel pushed himself out of the chair. "I thought college would keep TJ out of the war, but I was wrong. I thought I could keep him safe, but I was wrong about that, too."

He began walking toward the house. He looked old to me then, his shoulders sagging, his head low. Before he got to the back door, I called out to him.

"Colonel?"

He didn't turn around. But he stopped.

"Will you help Private Hollister?"

The question hung in the air, suspended between the whir of cicadas and the lonely coo of a mourning dove. I hugged my arms to my chest, as if I needed to hold myself up. Despite the heat, I felt a chill run through me.

"I'll think about it," the Colonel said.

And he disappeared into the kitchen.

That night I spread out TJ's Vietnam photographs on my bed. The soldier in the wheelchair, the bandaged stump of what had been his right leg pointing straight at the camera. A terrified child, naked to the waist, hands to his ears, running down the road, a helicopter hovering in the distance. The soldier on the stretcher, the wound soaking his bandaged chest. A hollow-eyed GI staring at the camera, the skin burned and scarred across his cheeks and forehead.

I left them all on the Colonel's desk, fanned out like a hand of cards, where he would find them in the morning when he sat down to drink his coffee.

fourteen

School started the Tuesday after Labor Day. If I'd had any big dreams about the eighth grade being some kind of promised land, they fell flat pretty quick. Eighth grade was just like seventh grade, but even more so. Math was good, English was boring, and in history we were studying the Greeks and Romans, just like we had in seventh grade and sixth grade, too.

The one bright spot of my day was newspaper. Sixth period, Mrs. Ronco's room, second floor. Originally my elective had been Music Appreciation, but I'd met a new girl in first period pre-algebra class, Alice Freeman, who complained that she couldn't be a staff photographer for the paper because she didn't know how to develop film.

"Why don't you learn?" I'd asked her. "I could teach you."

"I'm allergic to the chemicals," Alice told me. "At least I assume I am. I'm allergic to almost everything else. Anyway, my mom won't let me get near a darkroom, just in case."

So we hatched a plan. She could take pictures, I would develop them. And wonder of wonders, Mrs. Ronco liked our plan just fine. The only catch was, I'd have to write articles for the paper too.

"I can't write," I told Mrs. Ronco. "Just ask every English teacher I've ever had."

"It takes practice, like anything else," Mrs. Ronco insisted. "Besides, the beauty of newspaper writing is that there's a formula to it. Just follow the rules and you'll be fine."

Well, rules I could do. So I wrote my first article, which was about a new teacher who had been teaching in India for the last three years, and it turned out okay. Alice took the pictures, and they turned out even better.

"Look at this, it's got my byline," I told Private Hollister, slapping down the paper on his desk. He was still at the rec center, still waiting to hear if he'd be shipped out to Vietnam, but so far, nobody in his unit had gone as far as the Dairy Queen in Harker Heights. The new guy from Fort Sill had yet to arrive to take over the rec center. So Private Hollister stayed put, mopping up and reading comic books.

"I didn't know you were a writer," he said after he'd finished the article. "This is real good."

"I'm not a writer," I insisted. "I couldn't write my way out of a paper bag. But newspaper reporting is different. You just put down the who, the when, the how, the where, and the why, and you've got it licked. There's nothing fancy to it."

"It's still real good." Private Hollister pulled a deck of cards out from his top drawer and waved them at me. "What do you say?"

"I don't know. I'd hate for you to get ahead of me."

Private Hollister pulled a pad of paper out of the drawer. "Look, a whole new record-keeping device. The notebook's retired. Nothing can ever change about how things ended this summer."

One game. August 29, 1969, the Friday before Labor Day. We'd started playing the minute I walked in, and we kept playing until five p.m., taking a fifteen-minute break for lunch. The day began with Private Hollister two games ahead of me, but by midafternoon we traded the lead with every hand.

"You got him right where you want him, now show him where the door is," Sgt. Byrd cheered from the pool table, where he was going through a stack of papers. He held one up to examine it more closely, and I realized he was looking at a photograph.

"Is that one of yours?" I asked him. Ever since he started helping me in the darkroom, I'd wanted to see some of Sgt. Byrd's photographs, but he never printed any. He only developed the film.

I put down my cards and walked over to where he was. "Can I see one?"

"Nothing to see, really," Sgt. Byrd said, but he handed me the picture all the same. It was of a soldier sitting in front of a hootch, clearly somewhere in Vietnam.

"I shot three hundred rolls of film over there," Sgt. Byrd explained. "And now it's all developed. So I thought I'd try printing some."

"This one came out good," I told him, admiring how the print's graininess gave it a sort of moody feel.

"Yeah, it's okay. But I don't know how many more I can do."

"How come?"

He let out a deep breath. "Too many memories. I look at all my negatives and I ask myself, why do I want to remember that?"

"Maybe you don't have a choice."

"Exactly, my dear Watson. That's the very conclusion I've drawn myself. I'm between the proverbial rock and hard place, memory-wise."

"You giving up on the game, Jamie?" Private Hollister called. "Because I'm still ahead, and that's fine by me."

I sat back down. And by four forty-five we were racing through the final hands. The person who reached one hundred points won the game, the set, the match, the whole enchilada.

My last hand was a beauty. I was dealt two pairs off the bat and a run of three spades, the three, four and five. Every turn I picked up something I could use, discarded what I didn't need. But when I looked up at Private Hollister, I could tell the same thing was happening for him. Should I go ahead and knock? If I waited too long, he might get that last card he needed, might rid himself of all deadwood and get gin.

I knocked.

It was close. Very close. I spread out my cards on the desk. I had one unmatched card.

Private Hollister laid out his hand. Three pairs. The jack and queen of hearts. And two pieces of deadwood, cards that didn't match anything.

I'd won. By a card. On the last day of summer.

"Man, oh man," Private Hollister said, shaking his head. "You whupped me."

He wrote the points down in the notebook. And then, at the very bottom of all our scores, he signed his name and handed the notebook to me to do the same.

"You keep it," he said, when I tried to hand it

back to him. "Just so you remember all the good times we had playing. That's about the most fun I've ever had playing cards. It ain't fun unless you're playing with somebody who knows what they're doing."

I could have cried. I didn't, but I could have.

Now I eyed the deck of cards, wondering if it would spoil things to ever play gin rummy with Private Hollister again. Maybe I should leave the memory of my amazing victory in pristine condition, unmuddied by any later losses.

Oh, what the heck. I took a seat across from Private Hollister. "Deal 'em," I ordered.

For a while I checked in at the rec center two or three times a week, sometimes hanging around to play cards, other times just stopping in to wave and then heading on to somewhere else. School was running me ragged. Mrs. Ronco kept assigning me newspaper articles, and it seemed like I was doing everybody's darkroom work for them. Alice Freeman said she bet our newspaper would win some sort of prize for photography, I did such a great job making the pictures look good.

At first, every time I stopped by the rec center, my heart beat a couple beats faster right before I walked in. Would Private Hollister still be there? The Colonel had never given me a direct yes or no about helping him, and I knew I shouldn't ask. It went against protocol to ask about a soldier's orders, and I'd done it once. I couldn't do it again.

But after a few weeks, I relaxed. It seemed clear that Private Hollister wasn't going anywhere. I relaxed so much, sometimes I went for a week without checking on him. Alice had started teaching me to take pictures using her camera. She thought it was crazy that I knew so much about developing and printing film and not a thing in the world about photography, which she informed me was the art of writing with light. We'd stay after school and take pictures of the football team, the lockers, the janitorial staff, all kinds of different stuff, just to see how interesting we could make it look.

One afternoon when I got home from school

there was a roll of film from TJ waiting for me. "Any letter?" I asked my mom, who was writing out a grocery list on the kitchen table.

"I don't know if he wrote you one. He sent a short one to Daddy and me. Not much news. He says he wants to learn to fly a helicopter."

Of course there was no letter in the envelope he sent me, just the film. I decided to go ahead and develop it that afternoon, and if I didn't have time to print it, I could take the negatives to school with me the next day and work in the dark-room there.

"Don't even ask me to play cards," I called out as I walked into the rec center. "I don't have the time. I've got a roll of a film to develop and a history test to study for. It's all about Greek columns, if you can believe it. Like anybody needs to know that stuff."

"I'm sorry, I'm not sure I follow you."

The soldier sitting at Private Hollister's desk was not Private Hollister. He didn't bear the least resemblance to Private Hollister. He was heavy-set and bifocaled and had a five o'clock shadow.

I wasn't sure if Private Hollister actually shaved more than once a week.

"Where's Private Hollister?" I asked, realizing it had been over a week since I'd seen him, maybe two. "He's supposed to be working here."

"Reassigned. I'm Private Grenier. Is there something I can help you with?"

"Reassigned where?"

"1st Signal."

"Here? At Fort Hood?"

"Not sure. He might have been with one of the units that shipped out to the Third Corps Tactical Zone last week."

"Vietnam?"

"Saigon or thereabouts. Place called the Parrot's Beak. Buddy of mine at Fort Sill was there. Said it was pretty grim."

Panic rocked me like a hurricane wind. I'd stopped paying attention and now Private Hollister was gone. I ran from the rec center and looked around wildly, as though maybe it wasn't too late, maybe there was still time to find him. But there was nothing to see, just the blank-faced buildings

that lined Battalion Avenue, typical Army archi-
tecture, nothing there to give you a plan for what
to do next, nothing to give you one single answer.

There was only one place I could go for answers,
and that was the chief of staff's office. If I wanted to
know what happened to Private Hollister, I'd have
to ask the Colonel.

fifteen

"He can't see you right now, honey. He's on an important phone call."

Miss Murlene, the Colonel's secretary, smiled at me and held out a plate of cookies. "Mama made these last night, special for Col. Dexter. She thinks the world of him. Take one; they're snickerdoodles."

I took a cookie and munched on it without actually tasting it. How could I have let Private Hollister get away from me? I counted back the days since I'd seen him last. Ten. Ten days. Anything could have happened in that amount of time. He could have been shipped out to Vietnam, killed, and returned to the States in a body bag in ten days, easy.

"You want to sit down, sweetheart?" Miss Murlene pointed to a row of hardbacked chairs lined up against the wall outside of the Colonel's office. "I don't know what his phone call's about, so I can't tell you how long he's going to be."

I sat down on the middle chair, taking another cookie from Miss Murlene. I immediately started fidgeting. "Are you sure you can't interrupt him?"

Miss Murlene shook her head sadly. "Oh, no, honey, you know how your daddy is. That's the number one rule around here: no interrupting Col. Dexter when he's on the phone."

"What if it was an emergency?"

"What's your emergency, honey? Did something awful happen at school? Awful things were always happening to me at school. One time I spilt orange-ade all over my new skirt at lunch, and I just cried and cried. My sister had to call Mama and tell her to come bring me a clean skirt, or else I'd just have to come home. Did you spill something on your clothes at school, darlin'?"

"No, ma'am. There's just something I need to know."

Miss Murlene smiled at me. "That's sweet, coming all this way to ask your daddy a question. You children really look up to him, don't you?"

"Yes, ma'am."

Miss Murlene turned back to her desk and began typing at machine-gun speed. Every few minutes she turned to see if the phone's red light was still blinking, and when she saw that it was she'd turn to me and make a big sad-clown frown. I liked Miss Murlene, but I realized that she was not necessarily the best person to have around in a crisis. Especially since she apparently couldn't recognize a person in a crisis situation when she saw one.

"He's off the phone!" Miss Murlene cried after I'd been sitting in that chair long enough for my rear end to go numb. She picked up the receiver and pressed a button. "Colonel? Jamie's here to see you, sir. Yes, sir. I'll send her in."

She turned to me and smiled like she'd just gotten me a date with Santa Claus. "Go on in, honey. He'll see you now."

When I opened the door, the Colonel was getting up from his desk, which was the size of a small car. On the wall behind him hung plaques in neat rows announcing his various awards and honors, and directly over his head was the 1st Cavalry insignia, needlepointed and framed by my mother, a shield with a black horse's head on the upper right-hand side, a black diagonal slash running beneath it, the background a yellow-gold. She made one for every post we were assigned. It was like having an embroidered history of the Colonel's career.

The Colonel didn't bother with any small talk or niceties when he saw me. "I'll take you home," he said, reaching for his briefcase. "Your mother is waiting."

"I didn't come here for a ride." I walked in and closed the door behind me. "I needed to ask you something. . . . It's about Private Hollister."

"It can wait," the Colonel said, coming around to the front of his desk and taking his cap from the coat rack. "We need to get going."

You can get to a breaking point with some people, and I had reached it with the Colonel. I had spent my entire life loving him better than anybody else in the world, and looking up to him and admiring him, but I'd just about had it. I'd tried not to hold it against him that all my life he'd told me the Army way was the best way, but when it came down to it, he hadn't done things the Army way at all. He'd done things the way everybody else did them: When he'd had a problem, he tried to take the cheater's way out. I'd done my best to overlook this fact once I'd learned it, but I'd had enough, now that he was giving me the runaround with Private Hollister. Like he actually cared about protocol. Like he actually cared about the Army way of doing things so much he couldn't tell me one way or another what had happened to my friend.

I slammed my fist on his desk. Hard.

"No, it can't wait! No, it cannot. You're going to tell me what happened to Private Hollister, and you're going to tell me right now. Did you sign those orders? Is he in Vietnam?"

The Colonel put his briefcase down. He put his hat on. "One dead boy in that family is enough," he said in a steady voice. "More than enough."

It felt like every muscle in my body went slack when I realized what the Colonel was telling me. "So you didn't sign the orders?"

He didn't say anything for a moment. Then, picking up his briefcase, he told me, "Your brother is missing. We need to go home."

It took me a full five minutes to comprehend what the Colonel had said. I'd followed him out of his office, past Miss Murlene's desk, into the hallway, down two clattering flights of stairs, and outside into the late afternoon heat, the parking lot still pulsing with it, the tires just minutes away from melting. I'd slid gingerly into the car, the leather seats still hot enough to burn, and clicked on my seat belt before I fully understood what the Colonel meant when he said my brother was missing.

He did not mean that TJ was lost in the super-market.

He did not mean that TJ had gone home to a friend's house after school and had forgotten to call.

He meant that my brother was somewhere in

Vietnam, but nobody knew exactly where, and nobody knew exactly what he was doing, or if he was doing anything at all. He might just be sitting there, on a half-rotten log in the jungle, a bamboo leaf tickling his ear, just sitting there and waiting for somebody to find him.

sixteen

Every last picture was of the moon.

I'd torn out of the Colonel's car the second he'd put it in park in our driveway and bolted back to the rec center. But once I'd gotten into the darkroom, I took my time developing the film, working carefully as I could so the negatives would be perfect, no marks, no scratches, nothing to get in the way of what I wanted to see. I believed those negatives would reveal the truth about TJ, what he'd been doing right before he went missing in action, what he'd been thinking about, some clue that would tell me where he was about to go.

Then maybe somebody could go and get him back.

There's a moment in the darkroom, when you hang your negatives to dry, that you finally see what occurred the moment you opened your camera's shutter to let in the light and make a picture. I was learning that half the time me and my camera had been looking at different things. I'd focused on Alice's face, but the camera caught the girl behind her combing her hair in the mirror. I took a picture of a tree bending in the wind; my camera found a bird taking flight from a branch.

Alice said that the best photographers saw what their cameras saw. They saw the girl in the mirror and the flying bird. What TJ and his camera had seen was the moon, thirty-six frames of it.

When I loaded the negatives in the enlarger and printed the pictures, I discovered that in some of them wispy clouds were sliding by a full moon's eyes, and in others crescent moons stood suspended in the night sky like slivers of light, Venus twinkling beneath them. There were quarter moons and waning gibbous moons, every sort of moon there was, sometimes with stars peeking out from the corner of the frames, sometimes framed by circles of light—which later, when I looked it up in the encyclopedia, I learned were called penumbras.

I printed every one of them, over and over. I blew them up until moons filled the frames. I blew them up until the only thing you could see were millions of tiny grains of light. Somewhere in there was a clue, I felt sure of it. For two days I printed the moons over and over again, my hands shaking, my heart racing. And with every picture I printed, I grew more and more afraid.

Because there were no clues. There was nothing but light and darkness, circles and crescents, a tiny star, a piece of a cloud.

When I was done, when I finally couldn't think of one more way to look at TJ's moons, I took them to Cindy's house. I wanted to show them to somebody who wouldn't feel afraid when she saw them.

"Is this my birthday present?" she asked me when I handed her the photographs. "Because it's my birthday tomorrow, only I'm not having a party. My mom says since TJ's lost we can only have a family party. Otherwise it would be bad manners to your family."

"You could still have a party if you wanted to," I told her, my voice flat. I felt as though my body had suffered a series of electrical shocks and now I was empty of feeling. "And then when TJ comes home you could tell him all about it."

Cindy shook her head sadly. "It's too late. My mom already called everyone and told them not to come."

"Do you want to hang up the pictures? It would be sort of like decorating for a party."

Cindy grabbed a roll of tape from a kitchen drawer, and we went upstairs. Thirty-six eight-by-ten moons take up a lot of space, and by the time we were done putting them all up on Cindy's walls, her room was covered.

"Did you know that some planets have lots and lots of moons?" Cindy asked me. We were sitting on her bed like a couple of planets ourselves, orbited by every kind of moon imaginable. "I thought my teacher was crazy when she said that to me, but then I asked Daddy and he said it was true. Satan has at least twenty-eight moons."

"I think you mean Saturn."

"And Jupiter has moons too," Cindy continued, ignoring me. "A bunch. But we only have one. But at least people can go to our moon. The other moons are too far away."

I wondered if TJ was looking at the moon right at that very minute, wherever he was. I wondered if he was imagining what it would feel like to rocket through space and land on the moon. To leave your footprints there. To cast a shadow across a crater.

It made me feel better to think he was.

Not much. But a little.

Private Hollister was sitting on the living-room couch when I got home. When he saw me, he stood up and said, "I heard about TJ being MIA. Byrd told me. Thought I ought to come see how you were doing."

I shrugged. I didn't even know how to answer that. "Okay, I guess."

We stared at each other for a few minutes, the silence as awkward as a turtle on its back. Fortunately, my mother, an expert hostess, came in and offered Private Hollister some iced tea, which he accepted. Then he turned to me and said, "You want to play some cards?"

"Sure," I answered, nodding, glad to have something to do besides stand there feeling stupid.

He looked to my mother. "Ma'am, would you like to play? It'll take your mind off of things."

To my surprise, my mother said yes. So when the Colonel walked in the front door about an hour later, there we were—me, my mother, and Private Hollister—eating peanuts and playing gin rummy.

"Colonel, this is Private Hollister from the rec center," I said. "Only now he's back at 1st Signal."

Private Hollister jumped up and stood at attention. "Private Bucky Hollister, sir. Pleased to meet you, sir." He saluted sharply.

The Colonel returned Private Hollister's salute and said, "At ease, soldier."

"What time is it?" my mother asked. "I haven't done a thing about dinner." She stood up and handed her cards to the Colonel. "Take my hand, sweetie. I've got a casserole that I've got to get in the oven if we're going to eat by seven."

The Colonel sat down in my mother's chair, examined his hand, and shook his head. "God knows I love that woman, but she collects dead-wood worse than a tidal pool."

Private Hollister laughed, then stopped abruptly, like maybe he thought laughing was disrespectful to my mother.

"It's all right to laugh, son," the Colonel said. "Mrs. Dexter's tough. She'd have to be, to be married to me all these years."

"Yes, sir. I mean, not 'yes, sir, it'd be tough to be married to you,'" Private Hollister stammered. "I meant 'yes, sir, I'll go ahead and laugh then.' Except I don't want to be rude, sir."

"You're fine, son. Don't worry about it."

"Thank you, sir."

"Whose turn is it, anyway?" the Colonel asked. "Because I need to get rid of some of this wood."

Private Hollister leaned forward. "No, I mean, thank you, sir. For what you did. I know it was because of you that I didn't get sent to Vietnam."

The Colonel raised an eyebrow. "How do you know that?"

"My CO told me you didn't sign my orders. You signed everybody's but mine. He figured it was because of my brother getting killed over there and everything."

"If you want to know the truth, I didn't sign your orders because my daughter asked me not to."

"Well, thank you, sir."

Then Private Hollister looked at me and grinned. "I sure am glad I let you win at cards."

I kicked him under the table, but he acted like he didn't notice. And then I looked at the Colonel, who nodded at me. And winked.

And that's when I knew that I'd finally made a good impression on him.

Or maybe I'd been making a good impression on him all along.

I like to think that's true.

We played cards all night, me, Private Hollister, my mother, and the Colonel, the moon rising behind us through the window, round and full. We played without keeping score, played just to hear the slap of the cards on the table, the riffle of the deck being shuffled. And though we didn't know it yet, somewhere in Vietnam my brother, TJ, was waiting in a prisoner-of-war camp, where he would wait for two more years, without a camera, without a pen to write us a letter to let us know where he was or if he was safe.

And when he came home, when the war was over, he would look at all the pictures I took of the moon while he was gone, one for every day, even on new-moon days, when the moon hung invisible in the sky, and he would stare at them for almost an hour until he finally said, *You got all the ones I missed.*

But we didn't know that yet.

ABOUT THE AUTHOR

Frances O'Roark Dowell is the bestselling and critically acclaimed author of *Dovey Coe*, *Where I'd Like to Be*, *The Secret Language of Girls*, *Chicken Boy*, *Phineas L. MacGuire . . . Erupts!*, and *Phineas L. MacGuire . . . Gets Slimed!* A veteran Army brat, she spent her formative years moving hither and yonder and is a former resident of Fort Hood, Texas, just like Elvis Presley. She lives with her husband and two sons in Durham, North Carolina.